# DECEPTION

## BOOK I OF THE SOLARI TRILOGY VOL. I

# SUNRISE

## SINTARI SUMMERS

Printed in the United States of America

First Printing, 2015

ISBN: 098613290X
ISBN-13: 9780986132902
Library of Congress Control Number: 2015904515
Starr Publishing LLC, Charlotte, NC

Starr Publishing
PO Box 28222
Charlotte, NC 28211
www.Starr-Publishing.com

Sintari Summers is donating a percentage of the proceeds from the sale of every book to the American Cancer Society.

Call your American Cancer Society anytime, day or night at 1-800-ACS-2345 for more information about breast cancer and to find out how you can join the fight against this disease.

This book is dedicated to anyone that ever believed in me…

# DECEPTION

de.cep.tion (di-sep'shen) n: 1. The use of deceit. 2. The fact or state of being deceived. 3. A ruse; a trick.

# TABLE OF CONTENTS

# PROLOGUE

# I

# THE PAST
# LONDON, ENGLAND
# TUESDAY, MAY 12TH 1812

An omen is a sign or indication that predicts good or evil. This is terminology used by logical people to describe the virtues of an omen, because for the superstitious, an omen is a fact representing the dreadful times ahead. So when an omen presents itself, then a catastrophic event precedes it, the logical person deems it a coincidence.

But on the contrary, a superstitious person is not surprised because he or she expected the tragic turn of events. Logic and superstition are a direct contradiction in terms. With this logic in mind, does that henceforth make the illogical psyche of a superstitious person indeed logical? Or could the mentioned unfortunate events be the chaotic world struggling to organize itself into a resemblance of order?

The coach driver must have belonged to the conglomerate of illogical superstitious people because he took the owl's hoot as an omen. The hoot's echo reverberated off of the brick facade of the small London towns' buildings and could even be made out over the rhythmic thumping of the horse hooves on the abandoned cobblestone street. What alarmed the coach driver most was not the loud animal cry, but the fact that there was no owl to be seen anywhere in the immediate vicinity. As the driver's heart decelerated back to its usual steady beat he observed his surroundings.

The night was late, but the moon—which appeared more than just full—illuminated the path ahead. As midnight approached, respectable people had performed their business of the day and were in bed. Thus leaving the streets empty. As the coach abandoned the cobblestone for a dusty pine needle path, the tiny London village became a dark deserted forest. The scent of decaying vegetation filled the air along with the spring rain's mist from earlier in the day. It was cool, giving the coach driver goose bumps.

At their leisurely pace the two horses continued. But the driver, accustomed to their demeanor, sensed their unease. He scanned the forest on both sides. The driver neither saw any danger, nor perceived a sound other than the horses' steady progress. The air was thick with the humidity from the earlier rain, along with an unpalatable tension.

When the driver caught an owl's hoot this time he jumped out of his skin. Thankful no one could see the sudden rush of blood to his cheeks the driver thought that he needed to calm his nerves soon. He dreaded having a heart attack if one of the thorough-bred steeds broke wind.

He wiped the cool sweat from his brow. The coach driver wondered if his passengers were as jumpy and apprehensive as he was.

There was still no sight of the innocuous bird of prey.

Inside the coach the atmosphere was just as thick as on the outside. This tension was not due to the weather, the darkness of the forest or the perceived omens; but because of the conversation between a man and his son. Father and child.

"But Dad, I want to stay here," the child's eyes pleaded as he said this to his father. He couldn't have been more than eleven or twelve years old.

"It is not up for debate," the young boy's father responded in Arabic. His deep baritone was delivered with calm authority, yet affection.

"But I don't want to go to Egypt," the boy continued begging.

"Son, I understand that," the child's father continued in Arabic portraying his anxiety, though his features remained an elusive mask. "But you must understand that it will be much safer for us there, amongst our own."

"What about Elizabeth?" the child said as tears welled up in his eyes. "And Mr. and Mrs. Tchaikovsky and Lenin and—"

"Enough!" exclaimed his father with a vicious look on his face. The child did not jump, though startled. He'd seen his father's rage and wrath on other occasions; though it was never directed at him. He composed himself before continuing, "Your mother and I have sheltered you far too long." The boy's mother, who had been sitting next to him, opposite his father, placed her hand on his hand with love as the child's father spoke. She looked with affection into his father's blazing eyes, warning him to be gentle. "No Ann," which was short for Andromeda. "It's time his eyes were opened." Turning to the boy, "Son, there has been a war brewing for quite some time; us versus them. Although it has been under a cloak of peace, they have now tipped the balance. The Prime Minister Spencer Perceval has been killed, that is the first time that they've ever been that bold. I don't expect you to understand, but you must try." He paused, formulating his next words.

"Proxima is dead with a host of our other relatives. They started this and won the first battle, but we must win this war by any means. And Elizabeth, her family," he paused making sure his son absorbed the full impact of his words. "All of them are our enemies. I know you were friends," he said before his son could interrupt. "But there are no friends in war. Though they have not participated so far, they will eventually. And there's no secret which side they'll choose."

He chose his next words with care. After a pause, his father looked him in his eyes and said, "Son, you must grow up fast because I don't know how long I will be here to protect you." The man's eyes became radiant and glowed with anger. "If you ever run into any of their kind again, kill them! Not just for yourself, but for your descendants. . . and for me. Show no fear, and fight them with every breath you have in your body! Then when you feel like there's nothing else, give your all, because they will show no mercy just because of who and what you are. I know you have it in you to make me proud, and I don't doubt that you will. Show no remorse, because you fight not just for you or me, but for a whole generation; for every single one of your kind. Avenge the death of every one of us who have fallen or will fall. Promise me!"

The boy, though reluctant, promised. His father had ingrained in him a sense of pride so deep, he'd never break a promise. No matter how frivolous.

The boy was aware of the owl's hoot too. It had an ominous undertone to him also. Not because of the present dilemma he and his family were in now. Not because of the quietness that engulfed the lone stage coach. But it was an omen marking the death of his youth and naive views of the world; the death of his innocent childhood. The omen signified the birth of the hardened man he'd grow to be.

As he looked out of the stage coach window, the light of the full-moon caused the tears on the boy's dark face to glisten, reminiscent of a many faceted diamond. They'd be the last tears shed for the rest of the boy's long life.

# II
# THE PRESENT
# ATLANTA, GEORGIA
# SUNDAY, MARCH 6TH 2011

"Tiffany, girl you sound like a hater," the young woman said to her friend. She was a very beautiful female with a creamy banana complexion. The form fitting Dereon skirt framed her body, showing off her ass. . .ets. Her pink halter-top hugged her double D breasts as a missed companion would. It matched her purse and stilettos to perfection. She had a face any southern gentleman could love, with pouty lips, high cheek bones and artificial hazel eyes. Her hair, done in African styled kinky-twists, accentuated her beauty. Her outfit showed most of her body; her long unblemished legs, flat cute tummy and well-rounded shoulders. Regardless, a hefty bag couldn't make her any less attractive.

"I'm not hating!" Tiffany replied with a smile on her face. She was nice-looking too, though not as pretty as her counter-part. "I'm just telling you all that being a player stuff is going to catch up with you Courtny."

"You sound like a hater to me," Courtny said and they both began giggling. The women were walking home from a party at the Complex in downtown Atlanta. It was approximately three o'clock on a Saturday night and though the city was still rowdy, the residential areas were calm.

The girls' heels echoed along the street as they walked and chatted. It was a warm spring night. Other than the occasional car or cab passing, the women were alone. Immersed in their conversation, they didn't appear to notice that the quarter moon did little to chase away unwanted shadows.

"Did you see the way Jermaine was looking at y'all?" Tiffany asked.

"Of course. He was jealous of the way I was twerkin' this thang on KB," Courtny replied, stopping a moment to do an impromptu dance demonstration. "You know how I be drivin' them dudes crazy," the sweet young woman continued. Her cockiness bordered on the edge of conceited arrogance. But she had reason to be all that and more.

"Yeah, yeah," said Tiffany, still hating on the down low. "I love those Morris Brown parties. They're always so live." The women both attended Clark Atlanta University and had just left a party at the other campus.

"Did you see when the Kappas came in stepping?" Courtny asked.

"Yeah, Jermaine nearly tripped looking at you." replied Tiffany with a fit of giggles. "I don't see what you see in hood dudes, they ain't nothing but trouble. Keep messin' with KB, and soon you'll be *In Too Deep* like Omar Epps." Both of them laughed even more. They continued to converse as they walked, and before long they were outside Tiffany's apartment building.

"Well girl, I'll holla at you tomorrow," Courtny said.

"Are you sure you'll be alright?" Tiffany asked, concerned about her friend who would be walking the rest of the way home alone.

"Girl it's only two blocks. Plus you already know, tool on deck." Courtny said as she patted the purse at her side. The girls giggled yet again.

"Girl you gone hurt yo'self," laughed Tiffany.

"Or somebody," retorted Courtny.

"Are you still gon' come over here tomorrow?"

"Hell yeah, I need to get my stilettos from you. Plus we need to go over Professor Rowan's notes. He'll probably have a quiz for us Monday."

"Yeah, you're probably right," Tiffany conceded. "Then call me as soon as you get home so I know ain't nobody crazy done snatched yo wild-ass up." Tiffany said joking, but serious.

"You're right too; Jermaine looked stalker-ish." The girls laughed again, and then they hugged and separated for the night. Courtny watched Tiffany enter her building before she started to head home herself. She hadn't taken ten steps before her Galaxy rung. Assuming it was Tiffany being paranoid, she answered without looking at the display, "Girl lay yo scary ass down, I'll be alright."

"That shit was foul," said a deep baritone into the cellular device.

"Boy stop. Jermaine you had your chance, now I've moved on," Tiffany said only half meaning it. She still had feelings for him, but KB, who was a successful drug dealer, took much better care of her financially. Until Jermaine became the accountant he was going to school to be, she had no use for him aside from sex. And she could get that when she wanted.

"I love you, and I know you love me. So why are you doing this?" His voice was pleading.

*Same sad story*, she thought. "Look, I'm on that Chris Brown Deuces shit. I suggest you get like me."

"So I'm not good enough now because my Chevy's not on twenty-eights?" Jermaine asked, guessing the reason she betrayed him.

"So what are you trying to imply, I'm materialistic?" she asked knowing he was.

"I don't know, are you?" Jermaine turned it around to her.

"You've got some nerve! I'm so through with you," she managed before hitting the end button on her phone. What he said didn't hurt her. It was the fact that she knew it was true.

Rap videos and BET convoluted many of today's young black communities' views and priorities. But today's generation is too uninformed to change its ways. Meanwhile, Lil' Wayne is in the rap videos with twenty half-naked women, in front of a Lamborghini, with thousands of dollars worth of jewelry on throwing cash. The males are imitating this, while the females are trying to be the next Karrine Steffans AKA Super Head. The sad part was that none of this crossed Courtny's mind. She was just concerned with the fact that KB didn't have *twenty-eights*. . .he had *thirty* inch rims.

Courtny continued down the deserted Atlanta sidewalk after she had placed her phone back into her purse. Not only did the air smell of spring, but of air pollution and garbage too. But she grew accustomed to it. On the other hand, the quiet of the streets unsettled her. A lone crumpled newspaper rolled along the street resembling an tumbleweed in the wild-wild west. Thoughts of her relationships and school filled her mind to the exclusion of everything else. So deep in contemplation, she jumped when suddenly a man was in front of her.

"What time is it?" he asked in a scratchy voice. She figured she must have been looking in her purse, that's why she nearly collided with him. She began to appraise his haggard look. Then she jumped more than when she realized he was in front of her.

He wore a long, tan trench coat that looked comical. It was so dingy it appeared brown. His Levi jeans were threadbare enough to reveal the stark white skin beneath them. His boots smelled like they were salvaged from a dump. Unbeknownst to her, they were.

Courtny dismissed him as a crackhead and started to continue her journey. The man repeated to her backside; which looked tasty to him and he admired, "Do you have the time?"

Courtny realized that the man was not a junkie searching for a fix, or someone to rob to get a hit. She turned to him and said, "No, I don't have a watch." She turned her wrists to show him. He nodded his comprehension, and then she turned to finish her stroll home. She anticipated her pillow and sheets like a child did Christmas. She was tired, which added to her weariness, making her more jumpy.

Her cell phone rang again. The sudden noise in the otherwise quiet night caused her to take a deep breath. She ignored Jermaine's call and took a few more cautious steps. That's when she realized that she had the time on her Galaxy and could have told the wandering smoker.

Courtny turned around and started to reach into her purse to get the phone and tell him, but the man in the musty trench coat was no longer behind her. The street appeared deserted once again. Feeling she went a little too heavy on the gin, too light on the juice, she chalked the eerie situation up to the long night of partying and bullshit.

Once again turning to head home, she screamed when she heard the noise in the alley to her right. Right away she looked in that direction. It relieved her when she saw a grimy looking cat foraging in the weekend piled garbage for a midnight snack. She took a deep breath. *Damn, this ain't Elm Street,* she reflected. Considering the circumstances, if it was, the black girl would die first. Unlike in the movies, she wouldn't—by any means short of the will of God—fall. That mentality along with the extra weight of her purse lingered in her head.

Just then, she felt herself jerked to her right in the direction of the alley as if by an invisible bungee cord. Scared now, she became terrified because the alley had just been deserted. She now realized that the watch-less fiend was dragging her to the abandoned alley to do who-knows-what. *I look too good for him to be just man handling and raping me,* she assured herself. In her state of fear, his grip on her arms felt inhuman.

He had his victim in the deep recesses of the alley. This obscured the view from any extra curious passer-bys. Next, with extreme force, the man slammed Courtny up against the wall of an adjacent building. Shrouded in darkness, a shaft of light from a passing car caught his face. Courtny, in her superficiality, had dismissed the man as being irrelevant just based upon his clothes. She had never registered his facial features. Now she did so in spades. His nose was too narrow for his pasty white face and he had a large angry mouth. His two-day old stubble made his demeanor even more menacing. He had deep blue eyes that sunk into his skull, giving them the facade of a murky ocean.

As Courtny took in his visual onslaught, he too appraised her with more than open adoration. He looked at her as if he was a hungry lion on the prowl who stumbled upon a plump gazelle. This caused Courtny to squirm, making her uncomfortable in her own skin. His hands were holding her biceps firm against the wall, one in each hand.

"You, *Miss I-Don't-Have-The-Time*, by now should realize that it's time for a snack." After saying this, the super-strong bum/crackhead licked Courtny on her neck. She shuddered with irrepressible revulsion that caused her to just about gag from the putrid stench of his breath. Fear was the only thing that kept the bile lodged in her throat. That and the use of other refined skills helped her repress her gag-reflex.

Throughout this humiliating exchange of bodily fluids, Courtny had been panicking as she foraged through her purse. It wouldn't have helped to reach her Galaxy. By the time she called 9-1-1, the assailant holding her hostage would have done whatever he had in mind. Whether it was robbery, assault, rape or... Courtny didn't want to contemplate it any further. Raised in the 'hood', and a single independent woman, Courtny had never depended on the police for a damn thing. So relieved when she found what she searched for, her tormentor noticed her obvious change in demeanor.

She looked at her hand, which was still in her purse. As she did, with arrogance, the man proclaimed, "Mace won't save you now banana pudding." He was referring to her smooth skin that resembled the dessert.

Courtny said, "It won't save you either mother-fucker!" after finding her heart. With that, she shot the concealed Browning Hi-Power nine millimeter semi-automatic pistol through the thin fabric of her purse. Bam!

In the confined darkened space, the muzzle flash was bright, blinding Courtny for a moment. The reverberating echo kept her from hearing due to the loud report. Uncertain if the man was screaming in pain, she was sure he was still holding her against her will.

Bap, bap, bap. . . She continued to squeeze the two pound tension trigger unaware of the dislodged shells that were burning her hand in the purse. Courtny continued to fire until the breech locked back on an empty chamber, signifying an end to the deadly weapon's assault. At this close range, Ray Charles was sure to find his target. So Courtny was positive that all nine bullets, eight in the magazine, and one loaded into the chamber earlier entered the man's midsection.

As the gun smoke cleared, the sting of it in her unprotected eyes wore off. The shock of having just shot a man nine times, maybe even killing him wore on. This must have been how the person who shot Fifty Cent felt. Far from coherent, she still wondered if the blood of the man had ruined her outfit. Yet once the smoke had dissipated, Courtny's mind was reeling. She now realized that the pressure on her arms had never gone away. And what she had assumed was screaming during her aggravated assault, turned out to be laughter.

The man was right in front of her, except now he was laughing as if Richard Pryor was back alive doing stand-up comedy. With his oblivious laughter, Courtny better evaluated his face; more so his mouth. He was unlike any fiend she had ever seen, because this man had perfect porcelain white teeth. With his head leaned back letting his laughter free, she had a perfect view of all thirty-two of them.

Albeit slow, his humor abated. He now looked her square in the eyes. As she returned his glare, the blue of his irises appeared to be taken over by his pupils. She thought it may have been a trick of the murky yellow street light reflecting off of a window or something. They became black as if the color evaporated out of them. He smiled as he said, "I like them feisty—especially the red-bones." Then she noticed how his canine teeth extended to an impossible length. The faint light glowing off them made the teeth seem surgically sharp.

Now, far surpassing scared, she was in a terrified state so advanced her whole body froze. She dropped her purse, leaving it to hang free from the thin strap on her shoulder. Courtny was not superstitious, nor did she trust in myths or fairy tales. But she now felt that Bram Stoker may not have been a fiction writer. She now knew how the guy that shot Fifty Cent *really* felt, once he realized his victim survived and still talked shit as this inhuman bum/crackhead vampire did.

"You should have used silver," he said as he went in toward her neck with his grotesque mouth opened wide. Frozen with fright, all she could do was accept the inevitable. A deer in the headlights.

"Sorry to interrupt, but can I have this dance?" a deep voice cut through the silence of impending doom, bringing Courtny back from her daze. She turned in the direction in which the retort came. The maniac crackhead/vampire/psycho-bum did the same thing. Frustration was obvious on his face from the interruption.

"Mind your business ass-hole," he said. Courtny and her attacker were both straining to see the new arrival. He was at the face of the alley, masked by its darkness, and silhouetted by the light of the street lamps. He was twenty feet from where Courtny and her newly anointed target range were. His features were indistinguishable. However, his voice, which carried exceptionally well in the silent night, was very conspicuous with its menacing intent. When he spoke, what he said was a promise, not to be misconstrued as a threat.

"Let her go and you'll die quickly." His eyes could be seen and they glowed red as if he had just been captured in a picture with the light reflecting off of his cornea.

"Or else what?" The musty smoker holding Courtny replied clichely.

"Or else," the man chuckled, "you won't die quickly." He said this surely.

"Who the fuck do you think you're talk—" the insane direlect started, but never finished. As he spoke, he had unconsciously released Courtny to turn and face this new challenge. As soon as he did, an extremely bright light exploded from the end of the alley where the man was. Courtny put up her hands to shield her eyes. Even behind her hands and closed eyelids, she could still feel the heat of the light coming from the mouth of the alley. When she felt—more so than saw—the light diminish, she opened her eyes. There was still a blur and dizzying circles in her vision, but she no longer saw her attacker and apparent rescuer. They were so suddenly gone, that Courtny wondered if they were ever there in the first place.

No more Grey Goose, she thought. Then she saw the tattered remains of her faux-Gucci purse hanging at her side. She reached into it and felt all of the empty shell casings. Perplexed, she walked calmly yet cautiously to the head of the alley and was now back on the sidewalk in the same place she was when she had originally been abducted from her homely pursuit and subjected to. . . She didn't know what.

Courtny looked up the street to the east, then to the west. The area was still as deserted as it had been five minutes ago. There was no sign of the evil fiend, nor her knight in shadowed armor.

Kneeling down, she undid the straps to her stilettos and slowly took each of them off. She stood up with one heel in each hand, and peered around with nervousness one more time. Sure that she was alone, Courtny took off like Flo Jo out of the blocks in the '96 Olympic Games. With the intent of winning not a gold, but platinum medal, she ran full-speed home and never looked back. She ran as if Freddy Kruger, Jason, and Michael Myers had formed a horror legion of doom; and they were all a hair's breath away from giving her eternal nightmares in hell. . . And she never slipped, stumbled or fell.

# DECEPTION

## BOOK I OF THE SOLARI TRILOGY VOL. I

### SUNRISE

*"Pensez le matin que vous n'irez peut-être pas jusques au soir, Et au soir que vous n'irez peut-être jusques au matin."*

*"Be aware every morning that you may not last the day, and every evening that you may not last the night.*

—ENGRAVED PLAQUE IN THE CATACOMBS OF PARIS

*"Of all the beauties in the known universe, nothing rivals that of the utterly simple yet splendid sunrise."*

—CENTAURI

# DAY ONE

# I
# LIFE IS PRECIOUS
# MONDAY, MARCH 7TH 2011
# SUNRISE: 5:32 A.M.

Life is very precious to those who still possess it. From the moment you are born, with each breath you are taking a constant step toward your inevitable grave. Though death is a release from the daily pain and suffering of this mortal world, many look at it as a punishment. So people in general are not in a rush to pass on and find themselves in an afterlife that will undoubtedly be filled with more pleasure than this ephemeral realm is convoluted with suffering.

A second is all the time it takes to have a life altering thought. A minute is all the time it takes to decide to act on an impulse. An hour is all the time needed to sow the violent seeds of discord that will irrevocably change your life forever. A day is how long it would take to realize that had you not acted on that original thought, the tragic events preceding it would have never occurred. A week can change your world and everyone around you to the point to where life's not worth living. And two weeks can start a downward spiral putting an end to the hectic and chaotic universe as we all know it; also a beginning to the prophesied hell of Revelations.

The distinct wail of the alarm clock cut through the silence of the room, alerting the occupant of the bed to its existence. It only alerted him and didn't wake him because he had already been up; reliving the past twenty-four hours of his life in a waking dream. Or nightmare.

He opened his eyes before he reached out and put an end to the distinct protest of the Sony device, then turned and sat up in bed. The alarm clock display glowed neon red, announcing the time to be 5:30 A.M. The man sat on the edge of his bed a moment before getting up and pulling back the drapes that concealed two floor to ceiling windows. He had chosen this apartment for that exact eastern facing view. The skyline of Atlanta was before him, and as he stood there, the sun slowly ascended from its nightly retreat. Its radiant, bright red glow shined the tarnish off of a silver sky.

After another moment of reflection, the man walked down to the first floor of his studio apartment to begin his daily ritual. There was a padded makeshift arena taking up his entire living room. He never had any company or anyone to entertain, so the space looked like a mini- dojo. Now standing naked in the center of the ring because that was how he had gone to bed, he struck a pose and focused before he began his sparring.

He did this every morning for as long as he knew how; as long as he could remember. It helped him unwind from a long night and prepare to take on a long day. He performed Tai Chi poses, stretches, techniques and exercises that kept his body firm and his mind open. The tension was worked out of his limbs and as the sweat poured from his sleek hairless body, he was able to momentarily forget his waking nightmares.

Kick, punch, kick. By focusing exclusively on performing the slow controlled body movements and postures with grace and poise, the mind achieved a calm empty clarity. Regular practice increases flexibility and strength, and improves cardiovascular fitness.

Frozen in place with his leg extended fully, the man looked at ease. He looked to have mastered how to control his body, even though he could not control his world.

After an hour of this, more relaxed than when he started the man went back upstairs and headed into his bathroom. He turned on the shower. Once he'd adjusted the nozzles to the desired temperature, he found himself under the water, letting it cleanse him of any stress his martial arts foray had left remaining. He washed without haste, making sure to thoroughly purge himself of sweat and the grime that had accumulated. After a shave of not just his face but of his head, the man stepped from the shower invigorated.

He grabbed a towel from the rack that was concealed by the dissipating steam. After a quick rubdown he threw it into the dirty clothes hamper. Once he had brushed his teeth then deodorized and oiled his body, he was back in his bedroom.

The bedroom as throughout the studio, had hardwood pine floors. The only objects in the room were the very sturdy built brass canopy bed, oak dresser and matching night stand on which his alarm clock sat. There was no television because the man had no time or interest in entertainment. He walked to the lone dresser and retrieved white Calvin Klein boxer-briefs, a pair of black dress socks and a Hanes tank-top under shirt. He put these items on and then headed to the door in the corner opposite the bathroom. Upon opening the door it revealed a very spacious walk-in closet.

The man caught a glimpse of himself in the full-length mirror on the back of the door as it swung open. He was an inch over six feet tall. His extremely muscular body carried the two hundred and three pounds with grace. His skin was a luminous milk chocolate shade, and beautiful enough to make most Cover Girls jealous. He was hairless except for the customary places and his unblemished skin was uncommonly smooth.

His face wasn't extraordinary by any means but it was a far cry from normal. His head and jaw line were smooth due to regular shaving. They appeared to be sturdy and strong. His teeth were a pearly white, not all perfectly straight, but all accounted for. They were framed by stout lips that were a quarter shade darker than his skin. His nose was wide portraying his African background. However, it didn't dominate his face as some peoples did. His ears were unremarkable, with detached lobes and a small silver set diamond stud on his left side.

The thing that stuck out most, also demanding the majority of people's attention that was directed at him, was his eyes. If his ears were unremarkable, his eyes were the polar opposite. Physically he looked to be in his late twenties or early thirties. However contrarily, his eyes gave off a dignified impression of knowledge such youth could not possibly possess nor obtain—the windows to the soul.

His eyes could be any shade at any time, from light gray to deep black. Sometimes at the right angle, they were even a hue of crimson. At other times they were a light green or a smooth brown. At this present moment though, they were just plain hazel. Which wasn't common, but wasn't unexplainable either.

The closet was filled along each side with a variety of clothes ranging from expensive custom tailored suits, to common urban gear from the Underground Mall. The bottom of the closet was lined with the same range of diversity in foot fashion. After a serious decision he took a pair of creased black dress pants off of a hanger and put them on.

Then, in the same fashion, he did it with his choice of a cream-colored, silk Ralph Lauren short-sleeved button-down dress shirt. He opted not to button the top button though. He was suave, not a jerk. Next he retrieved a pair of black and cream Stacy Adams dress shoes off of the floor, then a black leather belt off the rack. He went back into the bedroom. While he sat on the bed, he put on and tied his shoes. Again standing, the man laced the belt through his pants and tucked in his shirt tail.

Dressed at last, he was ready to grace a runway with his presence, but would unfortunately have to settle for the Atlanta streets. Looking at the night stand, the clock read 6:54. He walked over to it, took his iPhone off the charger and checked for any missed calls or messages. Having none, he thought about his empty wrist. He took a walk to the rail overlooking the rest of the apartment, and then the man glanced down and spotted what he had been searching for. Next, he descended the hardwood stairs and headed into the small kitchen.

At his left was the living room he practiced Tai Chi in, to the right was his seldom used kitchen. Though his studio apartment was costly due to being in the heart of Metro Atlanta, its facilities were worth every penny. The kitchen housed a small dining table and four matching chairs. On that table sat his stylish silver fossil watch which people often mistook for being white gold. After he put on the time piece, the man went to his well accommodated side-by-side stainless steel Frigidaire. He grabbed a sixteen ounce single Sunny Delight then closed the door. That caused him to notice in the reflection, a slightly askew book on the bookshelf under the stairs. His was a well-stocked bookcase which lined the whole wall in that area. He walked to the shelf, seeing that the unorderly book in question was Robert Greene's *48 Laws of Power*. It was likely the last book he had been reading. The man corrected it and then headed towards the front door. He glanced at his watch, it read 7:03. He was on time. Snatching his keys off of the hook by the door, he left to begin what promised to be at the least an eventful, if not life changing day.

# II
# HAVES AND HAVE NOTS

THE WHITE CARGO VAN PULLED INTO A VACANT PARKING SPOT TEN FEET FROM THE
entrance to the Bank of America on Broad Street in downtown Atlanta,
Georgia. Simultaneously, the driver's door opened with the side sliding
cargo door. The driver waited as the two men in the back pulled out two
duffel bags carrying equipment and a ten pound bucket of paint. When
they joined the driver on the walkway, they proceeded to the entrance
of the bank.

It was obvious that they were painters. They each had on all-white
cover-alls smeared with the evidence of their trade. They also wore
painter's caps, goggles, latex gloves and dusk masks to protect their hair,
their eyes and mouths from the harmful vapors of the paint and paint
thinner.

They entered the large bank which was now being remodeled. They
noted the large overhead wall clock, it read 7:04. Wall Street trading
lines had been open for over an hour, so the business rush of customers
had dwindled. There were around seven in the lobby, and about as many
managers and tellers throughout the thriving business. On a Monday as
it was, the bank had been loaded with cash to appease those who had to
catch up from business done over the weekend when it was closed.

Fortunately, the driver of the van knew this—unfortunate for the
bank owner and its occupants. For some people, working for what you
want and saving until you are able to acquire it was alright. But for some,

there wasn't enough work or time in the world to gain what they wanted. Their worldly desires outweighed their legal ambitions.

So as the *haves* flaunted their good fortune in the *have-not's* faces, some got fed up. In the ghetto, the pursuit for riches was a multitude of people's motivation. Material possessions transformed from a want, to a need of more importance than the very air we breathe. People have killed in the hood for a ten-dollar rock of crack-cocaine before with no remorse whatsoever. So what do you suppose they'd do for a thousand dollars? Or ten thousand? What about one hundred thousand dollars? This very bank holds far more than that. More than someone out of the ghetto would ever see or spend their entire life. What would they do to achieve the riches fantasies are made of? You will find out shortly. Oppression is more than enough motivation for premeditated evil; evil in your mind, necessity in another's. Beauty is always in the eyes of the beholder.

The three men walked to the center of the lobby of the bank. The driver, who was shorter than the other two painters, took the bucket of paint and placed it on the counter used to write checks and deposit slips. The other two men each carried a duffel bag to an opposite, prearranged corner of the bank. They each kneeled down and unzipped the bag they had been carrying that held their tools.

So far the bank's customers had been oblivious to these men and their actions. Indifferent to them and their occupation, they didn't register as anything other than blue collar laborers coming to paint in their white collar world. *Good,* thought the driver. However, when they heard what the driver proclaimed, and saw the 'tools' that the painters held, they no longer worried if the Dow or NASDAQ was up one percent. They contemplated the percentage of escaping with their lives.

The two men who had accompanied the driver now each held a machine gun at waist level. One held a hefty AK-47 that looked weathered. With its fully loaded magazine of thirty 7.62 x 39 millimeter half-metal jacketed rounds, the lethal device weighed ten and a half pounds. Regardless of wear, it was still capable of delivering six-hundred rounds per minute. The other man held a SKU, the shortened version of the AK-74 which was the upgraded version of the original Auf Kalashnikov, circa 1947.

"May I have everyone's attention please," said the driver in a loud clear voice. Not everyone focused their eyes on him, but they did when he spoke next. Softly patting the ten-gallon bucket of paint, he continued. "This is a bomb, and if everyone does not do exactly as I say, I will blow this building and everything within a quarter mile radius to kingdom come." A few people gasped while some started to protest. Either way, by now they recognized the seriousness of the situation. The two men with machine guns helped.

Sure that everyone's eyes were now trained on him with rapt interest, he continued. "Tellers, if you pull any silent alarms or put any tracers, marked money, tracking devices or dye packs in the mix, everyone here will die." He said this with the false conviction and knowledge that if warned about the items, then bank policy kept them from disobeying. "Their blood will be on your hands. My cohorts and I have nothing to live for, so make my lifetime." As he spoke, the other two men took the now empty duffel bags to the tellers to have them filled with pirated green backs. When the men were at the tellers' partitioned stations, the driver started speaking again.

"Please help my friends graciously by filling those bags with the money we came here for." He spoke in a calm manner as if ordering a burger at Wendy's. The tellers complied with hesitation that would soon dissipate.

"I plan on placing a censor on the exits of this building so if you try to leave, you will die." Holding up a remote that had previously gone unnoticed in his hand, he said, "If the cops are notified before we have been gone ten minutes, I will detonate this bomb by remote and you will die. This money is none of yours; furthermore it's insured. There's no sense in any of you trying to be a hero. A man's worth begins when he is willing to die for his principles. I am. Are you? As long as you follow my instructions, you will be able to return home to your families safely later on today."

During this brief monologue, the bags were being silently and nervously filled. The only noise in the room, other than rapid breathing and the transfer of cash to be heard was the steady tick-tick sound that was coming from the bucket. With each tick it seemed one of the hostages anxiously jumped.

Good.

Other than that, nobody moved. They were deeply rooted in place by fear. Aware of their discomfort, the driver played on this perceived terror.

"This is five pounds of C-4 plastic explosives. It was manufactured in America, so it's guaranteed to be destructive. Our brilliant scientists took ionized plastique explosives, compressed and intensified them into this easy to carry and conceal package. Yet 1.6 million people will die of starvation and exposure every year. In the meantime the government is funding programs to develop these things used to kill, instead of trying to give life to the poor and needy. America, Obama can't save us by himself." He said this last part shaking his head in disgusted protest.

By now, his co-defendants' bags were filled and they were being zipped up and hoisted onto their shoulders. The driver looked at the clock once again, it displayed 7:06. If the cops had been alerted their sirens would have been able to be heard by now. The hostages hadn't snitched. The plan was on schedule and running smooth. Had the police come, the driver had a contingency plan; but it seemed he wouldn't need it.

After hoisting up the deceptively heavy duffel bags, the two accomplices dropped their machine guns. This startled the bank occupants who feared bullets would just randomly start spraying in every direction. Contrary to their fear, they did not. The weapons landed with a tandem hollow thump. The captives were scared to move. Much bigger problems than a few bullet holes seemed to wait on the horizon, keeping them distracted and complacent. There were no heroes in this group.

The lawless gang exited the bank with the two men carrying the money first. Before the driver followed, he kneeled at the swinging doors of the bank and attached two sensor-like objects he had produced from his pocket and placed them on each one. While turning back, his parting words to his captives were, "The bomb—which really isn't a bomb—will disable itself in thirty minutes if we are not pursued. I appreciate your cooperation, and I hope this 'brush with death' has made you evaluate your lives." When he said 'brush with death' he pantomimed air quotes.

"Think about it and everything else I said when you're driving in your luxury cars and pass a homeless person on the streets." With that, Robin Hood headed out of the door to join his band of merry men.

His accomplices were in the van with it started. The driver was exuberant when he slid behind the wheel. They were all laughing and prematurely congratulating each other when they were about to pull away from the recently robbed Bank of America on Broad Street. That was the street that they were in the process of turning onto. It was also the street that the sirens and wails of a police car seemed to be headed up—in their direction.

*Oh Shit!* the driver thought. By now, the other two robbers were panicking and shouting, "Drive, Drive!" into his ear. They were wondering why he hadn't pulled into the traffic, ahead of the impeding law to try to allude arrest. To their concern he just sat there, calm as ever.

They were just about to voice more protests when he spoke up, "Listen, calm down. I couldn't outrun a squad car in this van if I had NOS so I wouldn't try." He said this referring to the powerful fuel compound nitrous-oxide used to give drag-racing vehicles an extra boost of speed.

"So you're just giving up?" one asked incredulously.

"What even makes you think that they're after us?" the driver countered. The van grew quiet as the sirens grew louder. By now the light could be seen flying down the street in hot pursuit. The tension in the vehicle was palatable. The two men were on the verge of screaming mutiny. They had no intentions of having a shoot-out and even if they did, at the insistence of the driver they left the guns at the scene of the crime. Just as one of the men was about to jump out of the van with one of the bags of money and run, they could all see the black-and-white car was in full pursuit—however, not in pursuit of them.

The cruiser flew by them on Broad Street doing at least sixty miles per hour. You could see that the men in the back of the van were still tense, but they wiped the sweat that had accumulated from their brow while breathing a deep sigh of relief.

The driver, who had remained level-headed, calmly pulled off into traffic. His target was his new life funded with the spoils of this hectic and risky endeavor. Had he sped away to begin with, they would have been chased and caught, like most other criminals whose own guilt gave away their position. At least he was smart enough to know this—even if his co-conspirators didn't. The point was moot; he still had a plan B.

Now driving away more quickly than he should have, the driver and master-mind of the heist wondered if they would eventually be his downfall. Maybe he should kill them now to avoid any future trouble because they had proved that they couldn't think under pressure.

These thoughts were running rampant through his mind when just as suddenly they were forgotten. He saw the blue lights flashing in his rear-view mirror. Birchwood was always hot, and this time the police were in pursuit of them.

The driver's cell phone was in his hand. *Time to execute plan B,* he thought.

# III
# THE CITY OF MURDERED DREAMS

AFTER LOCKING HIS DOOR AND DESCENDING TWELVE FLIGHTS OF STEPS, THE MAN had emerged from his apartment onto the stoop in front of the building. He could have taken the elevator, but why would he, knowing that his legs worked perfectly well? That same mentality was the reason he was walking at this precise moment. Though he owned two cars, the man walked to work to gather the much needed and anticipated sunshine.

Atlanta. It is the capital and largest city in Georgia. It serves as the distribution, manufacturing and transportation center of the southeast. Located on the Piedmont Plateau in northwestern Georgia, it is the birth and burial place of the famous civil rights leader Martin Luther King Jr. Today it's one of the fastest growing urban areas, bringing tourist from all over the world; especially since hosting the 1996 Olympics.

Atlanta is a place where dreams are born, and many die just as quick.

The man's job was about five miles away and he enjoyed every minute of his stroll. Sipping his orange juice as he passed a variety of people, he wondered if they had any idea what was going on and if they had his deep insight on life. When you're born, you immediately start dying. Though some accept this fact more gracefully than others, it doesn't change the situation. It's a hard reality to deal with, but as true as America having a black president. This is just as hard for many to live with.

He admired the city and its citizens every day as if seeing them for the first time. On his daily walk to work throughout the weekday, he passed a variety of people. A few students at a bus stop on their way to a much needed education. Delivery personnel, police officers, mail men and sanitation workers were also often seen in the process of servicing the public. More often he came across lawyers and businessmen on their way to the courthouse or office. Women looked at him with open approval, while the men glared at him with obvious envy. He was handsome and he knew it, though he also knew how to fit in inconspicuously when the time arose.

The air smelled of fresh flowers after the much needed rain from the previous day. The atmosphere was perfumed with the scent of a conglomerate of trees that housed chirping birds. Their songs were overridden by chatter and the radios of passing vehicles with their windows down and the occasional honking horn.

Atlanta, a city of change and ambition.

The man thought about and absorbed all these collective stimuli as he arrived at the entrance of Starr Private Investigators. A business housed in a small building on 13th Street. As the man started up the few intervening steps, a white unmarked panel van sped down the street causing the man to shake his head.

Atlanta, it was just another day in the city of murdered dreams. Little did the man know one day could change your whole life.

Or end it.

# IV
# GOOD MORNING

THE WOMAN WAS SHROUDED IN A VEIL OF DARKNESS. BUT EVEN WITHOUT LIGHT, her beauty was still abundant. Her skin seemed to radiate an aura so powerful that she glowed. She was petite, but power was clear in the structure of her muscles. Though very feminine, she appeared dangerous in an exotic way. She wore a black lace thong with a matching garter belt. The man lying in the bed looked to be floating in the darkness, evaluating who he believed to be the perfect woman.

Her skin was the color of butter and just as smooth and creamy. She was about five and a half feet tall. Her tummy was flat, and her exposed breasts were an exquisite handful with small brown Hershey-kiss nipples that begged to be sucked. Her round waist hinted at the nice buttocks behind her. As she walked to the bed, the man became so aroused his member tented the thin sheet covering his nakedness.

When she reached the bed, she drew back the sheets and smiled in anticipation. The woman turned around and bent over, drawing her panties down her legs nice and slow. This gave the man an unrestricted view of the most splendid set of lips he had ever wished to kiss. They were smooth and devoid of any hair. They were moist with the woman's anticipation of intercourse. Thick white cream oozed from her womanhood and left a trail down her leg all the way to her pretty petite feet.

He grew more aroused. When she turned back to face him, he looked into her deep dark exotic eyes, which sparkled as they always

17

did. Her nose was the center of a perfect oval face, and it rounded off her pleasing look. It was pointed with a slight slope of beauty. Her hair hung long and straight down her back and exposed shoulders. It was a dark brown bordering on being black. However, he'd been close to it enough times to know that it was brown. He had smelled it enough to know it was luxuriously fragrant. He'd dreamed it was spread across his stomach enough to know it was soft.

Her lips—luscious—appeared to be swollen from a night of passion. Though the night hadn't begun, he knew this was their perpetual state. Her high cheek bones had a reddish tint that had to be a blush at his open adoration because she never wore make-up. He smiled, so did she.

She climbed atop him and rubbed his hardness against her entrance. That coated her opening with his pre-cum as she simultaneously coated his member with her own juices.

He clenched his jaw with the strain of keeping himself from exploding before he had even entered her. She continued to rub her labia and clitoris with his ready rod. It seemed she was getting immense pleasure from this lewd act alone. Just when he thought he might die of the constant torture, she suddenly impaled herself with him and relaxed her full weight on his pelvis.

He moaned with ecstasy. She cried with euphoria.

He placed his hands on her ample hips as she began rocking back and forth to the rhythm of a song that she must have known well. She was experienced in how to please a man, though it wasn't apparent from the tight, moist warmth of her insides.

Her breast danced to the same music of their rapidly beating hearts. He was dazed and hypnotized. Nothing on earth could ever feel this good. Not even in his wildest, unrestricted dreams. Her hands clutched his chest muscles. Not afraid of hurting him, her manicured nails dug deep into his raw flesh. The pain was a welcome reprieve.

She suddenly leaned over him. Her hair curtained their faces before she placed a violent kiss on his lips. Then another. And once more. Next she sucked his bottom lip into her mouth and massaged it with her tongue. As she did this, she rode him faster and faster in a frenzied pace. The sound of sweaty flesh against flesh combined with their own deep breathing. Heavy heartbeats reverberated throughout the empty room.

As her kiss turned from one of need, to one of passion, her pace slowed again. Their tongues caressed each other tenderly. Next, she trailed kisses from his cheek to his ear. Her warm breath gave him a ripple of excitement. She whispered into it, "Can you feel my cum running down your balls?"

He did, though he was too caught up in the throes of passion to reply. "I'm cumming again," she whispered in a contained scream and began to shake uncontrollably. He felt not just the tightening of her insides, but more of the love juice she had asked about. She still never stopped riding him.

"Is it good?" she asked. He nodded. "Is it good?" she repeated. He nodded more vigorously. "Tell me," she moaned into his ear driving him mad.

"It's fan—tast—ic," he barely managed to exclaim.

"Well then tell me you're cumming," she said increasing her pace. "Tell me because I want to know. I want to savor it." Her vulgarity excited him even more.

"I—I'm almost there," he stammered uncontrollably.

"Yeah," she replied coyly. "Cum for me? Please cum for me!" she begged.

"Its, I can feel it." The muscles in his neck grew taut.

"Alright," she said jumping off of him and crawling down his body. Just as suddenly, he was out of her pussy and in her mouth. She began to lick and suck every trace of herself and their passion off of him. This was too much. More than any mortal man could stand.

"I'm almost there," he said. She moaned against him, the vibration driving him mad. The orgasm in his loins built to an impossible climax.

"Mmm," she moaned. "Mmm, mmm," she continued.

Then he heard a vibration in his head. Right at the edge and he heard the buzzing yet again. More of a ringing this time. What the. . .

The man hit the alarm clock with the frustration of being interrupted and sexually deprived. It fell off the night stand, but it didn't cease to ring. The man realized it was his cell phone. He reluctantly answered it. "What," the man asked after hitting the send button.

"Wright, you're still asleep?" the person on the phone asked, but it was more of an accusation than an inquiry. It was his partner who undoubtedly in their pursuit to be the greatest homicide detective ever, had been up for a while. His partner's name was Detective Thomas.

"Obviously not if I'm on the phone with you," Wright countered. He looked for his bedside clock which was on the floor now, he asked "What time is it?"

Pausing to look at a watch, his partner replied, "7:22."

His alarm wasn't set to go off for another eight minutes. "What's the rush?" he asked. Wright didn't normally show up at the department's headquarters until around eight o'clock. Why was his partner waking him up early?

"Hurry and get dressed. There's been a 2-11," —police talk for a robbery— "at the Bank of America downtown about twenty minutes ago. And there are possible hostages."

"That's not our jurisdiction. Isn't that bank FDIC covered?" he asked referring to the Federal Deposit Insurance Company that insured the bank's money. "How can there be hostages if the robbery has already taken place?"

"No time to explain, get here asap. The captain wants to see you." With that his partner hung up. He did the same.

Confused, Homicide Detective Sergeant Danny Wright got out of bed right away and headed to the shower. His boxers caught on his arousal when he took them off. His partner's call did nothing to affect or delude the dream he had almost enjoyed. The one he wished was completed.

Thinking of his partner, Wright got into the shower. They had been partners for nine months now. He was thirty-five, while his partner was two years his junior. They were two of the youngest people on the force, causing them to be resented by their peers for their early success. They had accomplished things detectives ten years older hadn't. They achieved this through teamwork and an understanding of each other's independent skills. Where one was weak, the other was strong in that area and vice versa. They knew their roles and played them well with each other in crucial situations.

This was the exact reason that kept them from being kicked off the force. Each had been a loner, refusing to work with others or annoying their counterparts so that they refused to work with them. It was unacceptable in a job where your life rested in your coworkers hands. Furthermore, there were the individual issues of race. Affirmative action strikes again. Wright's partner was Puerto Rican. He was Italian.

After a quick shower, shave and tooth brushing, you could see Wright's Italian features clearly. He had dark, stylishly cropped hair and the olive skin stereotypically attributed to Italians. Wright was an inch or less short of the six foot inclination. He was built from constant weight lifting since high school, causing his one hundred and ninety-five pound frame to be all muscle.

His chin was sturdy with a slight cleft. His teeth were naturally white except for a few silver fillings. He had dark brown eyes, a broad forehead and a nose that ostentatiously centered his face. He was a rugged handsome. His body held many scars acquired throughout his career. His nose was slightly askew from having been broken before. He had a small knife wound on his throat from where it was almost slit. These imperfections are what made him human.

Hurriedly, he dressed in a customary detective's suit. Wright was strapping on his ankle holster that held his police edition snub-nosed thirty-eight special when the alarm clock startled him. After retrieving the device from the floor, he turned it off and sat it back in its appointed place. Next, he put on his shoulder holster with its Sig Sauer ten millimeter, followed by his suit jacket.

Dressed now, Wright grabbed his cell phone, keys and badge before heading out of the front door of his two bedroom-one bathroom duplex bachelor pad. He was ready to face what promised to be another eventful day of protecting and serving the innocent streets of Atlanta, Georgia. Unlike most, from experience, he knew that everyday could be your last.

# V
# BOURGEOIS

THE IMMACULATELY DRESSED MAN LOOKED AT HIS DESIGNER LOAFERS AS HE ENTERED the building. There was not a crack or scuff in his shoes from the forty minute walk. *I'm good,* he thought.

The man entered the small reception area of Starr Private Investigators—SPI for short—and glanced around. The lobby was tidy and well-kept with a lingering smell of Glade Plug-Ins mountain breeze in the air. There were two plush tan couches lining the wall to the left and right side of the door. They matched the richly colored carpet.

Behind each of the Brooks Brothers couches was a large window displaying 13th Street. In one of the windows, printed in white letters was *Starr Private Investigators* in a scrawling courier script. Beneath it there was a phone number to the business.

In the middle of the reception area sat a large pine table, with glass sections and gold trimming. On the table rested the latest magazine issues of *GQ, Business Management, Forbes, Vanity Fair, National Geographic, XXL* and *People*. To the left, there was a door that led to an office used as a storage closet. Beside that door to the right sat a small three quarters full Oasis water dispenser with cone paper cups.

Centered against the wall of the lobby was a large wrap around oak desk sitting low enough to display a woman in a chair seated behind it. The desk was neatly kept with pens, paper, stapler, phone and every other assorted item on it in an apparent order.

The woman was engrossed in something on the computer screen when the man entered looking as if he stepped straight out of the *People* magazine on the pine table. As soon as he appeared, she quickly stood up with the papers in her ring-less left hand and walked around the reception desk.

To the immediate right of the desk was a door labeled restroom. And to the far right was another wooden door with S. Starr printed on it in silver Geneva font. As he walked in the direction of the latter door, he was intercepted by the beautiful young woman from behind the desk.

She was about five feet, seven inches tall and around a hundred and ten pounds. She wore a powder blue knee-length skirt suit, with a mauve button down blouse and matching high heeled shoes. Her blouse showed ample cleavage. Not too much to be considered unprofessional, but enough to still be considered sexy. Her long black hair was held together in a bun on top of her head by two black chop sticks. She had pouty lips, but in an attractive way. She had skin the same color of caramel. Her dark brown eyes were framed by thin black designer—Gucci—glasses, held up by a cute button nose. She wore little jewelry outside of the small gold hoop earrings and tennis bracelet she had on now. He carefully looked at her. The man could see why people thought she resembled the b-list actress Meagan Good. *Good comparison,* he thought.

"Good morning Mr. Starr," she greeted the man in a silky, seductive voice.

Finally, we have a name for him. Her's was Jasmine Whitt, straight-forward enough?

The use of that name was the only thing that irritated him about his assistant/secretary/receptionist. He sometimes jokingly called her his 'assecreceptionist'. She was all the above. Jasmine greeted the clients and kept the lobby clean. She manned the phone, while typing documents and filing tedious paperwork. At times she even dropped off or picked up his dry cleaning or washed his car, which she had done over the weekend. She was an invaluable resource to the man she unwelcomely called Mr. Starr.

She had graduated from a small community college called Chattanooga State in the neighboring state of Tennessee when she was twenty-two. Then she had moved to Atlanta—she'd said—'for a change of scenery and a fresh start.' After reviewing her not-so-impressive resume, Mr. Starr had reluctantly hired her. She had been diligently keeping up with his business affairs ever since. That was over three years ago, but she still insisted on calling him Mr. Starr.

"Call me Shawnn," the man stated with care. "And good morning to you too Jazz," he returned, smiling and using her nickname. He looked at the clock on the wall above the reception desk, it read eight minutes shy of eight o'clock. Shawnn always arrived to work by eight, where Jasmine would have already been there thirty minutes at least and opened up preparing for another day. They were the only people other than the owner of the building with access to his offices.

She handed him what she held, which was a copy of the days *The New York Times, The Atlanta Journal* and the weekly edition of *The National Enquirer.* All of those papers he read religiously. He graciously accepted the load in his free hand.

"What's on the agenda?" Shawnn asked Jasmine.

She replied, "You have an appointment with a Mrs. Hamilton at 9:30 which she just made. Before you ask, no I don't know what it's about. She just said she wanted the earliest spot because it was urgent." —As they all said— "And at 1:30, Mr. Clark is coming to pick up the report you did for him. Be sure to have it ready," she finished flashing her pearly white smile.

"No mail or anything else?" Shawnn inquired.

Shaking her head, Jasmine responded, "No. Nothing that I can't handle for you Mr. Starr," with that, she turned and reseated herself behind her desk. No doubt to return to her adventures on facebook or playing spider solitaire.

Shawnn chuckled to himself as he turned to enter his office thinking about Jasmine and the use of the computer and his last name. He didn't mind either because she was always ahead of her work which wasn't much and she did a good—no great—job; she even ran the many errands for him that he didn't have time to do on her personal time. She indeed was a sweetheart.

Shawnn entered his medium-sized office. Next, he slid between two plush chairs that were for clients on that side of the large cherry wood antique desk. He sat down in his sleek, black leather rolling executives chair while laying the newspapers on the uncluttered desk. Shawnn threw the empty Sunny Delight bottle into the black wire-mesh waste basket in the far corner of the office. He pressed the power button on his Dell modem and switched on the eighteen inch flat screen monitor. The only other furniture in his office was a large black metal filing cabinet located behind him to his right. His law degree and investigators license were framed and hung on the wall to his right. To his left was a large window giving an unrestricted view to a parking lot. The view could have been better since it only displayed other area businesses and the adjacent bus stop on the corner of 13th Street and Parker Avenue, but it served its purpose.

He didn't crack the closed blinds, he raised them fully to allow the sun to drench the room in warmth and illuminating every surface with natural light.

He sat down. As the computer powered up he picked up *The National Enquirer* studying the front page. The headline read: "WOMAN SHOOTS VAMPIRE NINE TIMES BEFORE IT FLEES WITH A DEMON." He turned to the headlining article and began reading.

"Twenty-one year old Courtny Mason of Atlanta, Georgia, told *Enquirer* reporters that on Sunday, March 6th at approximately 3:16 A.M., she was walking home from a frat party. She and a friend (who declined to be interviewed) had attended Morris Brown College when she was attacked by a 'vampire crackhead in dingy Timberlands and a musty trench coat.'"

"She then produced an unregistered nine millimeter pistol (which she did not have a permit to carry) and proceeded to 'empty the clip on that muthafucka!' Courtny said the vampire/crackhead then laughed in her face with his 'hot-ass breath', before a black veiled demon appeared. Suddenly, they both disappeared in a very bright 'heat-light', after exchanging heated words."

"Courtny would not admit that she was scared. She was adamant that she 'held her own'. Her story coincided with the evidence. . ."

Shawnn stopped reading. Chuckling to himself, he wondered, *Who would believe some shit like that?* As he placed the paper aside he realized that the computer was now loaded.

He entered his user password when it prompted him, then logged onto the internet. He checked his Yahoo Instant Messenger account. Nothing. He then did the same with his MySpace, Google and Facebook inboxes to meet the same negative results. Nothing but spam. Zilch, zip, nada. He hadn't had a serious reply to the question he had posted on many internet avenues since he'd originally asked it. That was around nine years prior when he had first moved to Atlanta and opened up Starr Private Investigators.

He'd gotten replies when he lived in D.C., Memphis, Baltimore, Columbia and Dallas too. But maybe he's alone in Hotlanta— as the city was sometimes referred to—when he asks; "Where will the light lead us?"

He logged off of the internet and started reading *The New York Times*.

After more than an hour, Shawnn had read through three papers from front to back and he was now doing *The Times* crossword puzzle. "A seven-letter word for 'Blood-Sucker'," Shawnn pondered aloud to himself, referring to the clue for nineteen across. "My lawyer," he replied, chuckling. He always had an obtuse sense of humor and found himself laughing at the oddest times. 'Take the good with the bad, smile when you're sad. Be thankful for what you've got and remember what you had' was his motto.

His laughter was cut short when he remembered the article in The *Enquirer*. His smile receded while writing in the clue to number nineteen down, which was a four letter word for 'holds flowers'.

Around ten minutes later Jasmine buzzed him on the phone letting him know that Mrs. Hamilton had arrived for her appointment.

He glanced at his watch which read 9:24. Shawnn told Jasmine to escort her in.

Seconds later Jasmine opened the door allowing the woman to pass, showing her in. The woman was, he guessed, about 5'9, maybe a hundred and some-odd pounds if she was soaking wet. . .with a pocket full of quarters—no, bricks.

She was clothed in a red mini-dress that left little to the imagination. Well, it did because Mrs. Hamilton's frame was fairly thin to be nice about it. With fewer curves than a drag-strip, bluntly speaking.

Her skin wasn't pale but it wasn't healthily tanned either. The features of her face were contorted thought Shawnn, but he couldn't tell because it was overshadowed by a large red sunhat. At least she was color coordinated. She had a tiny black purse with a thin black strap draped over her frail, bony exposed shoulder. Her fiery red hair indicated that she may have been pretty if not for the huge sunhat. He could not see her eyes which had him slightly uneasy.

As Jasmine closed his office door Shawnn stood coming around his desk to shake her frail, cool, sweaty hand. He repressed the urge to wipe his own hand off on his pants legs or subtly grab a tissue.

"Shawnn Starr," he stated introducing himself. His smooth baritone carried throughout the office.

"Heather Hamilton," she returned with a calm southern drawl. She released his hand, pulling it away as if prolonged contact would contaminate her.

*Allergic to black people I see,* Shawnn thought, but didn't voice his opinion.

"A pleasure to meet you," she said, however Shawnn very much doubted it. "I have heard rave reviews about your services." He did believe that though.

"Thank you. Have a seat Mrs. Hamilton. Can I get you some coffee or something refreshing?" Shawnn asked out of habit. He knew manners were an overrated virtue only to those who didn't have them.

"No thank you. Your receptionist offered me some already Mr. Starr," she replied taking a seat in the chair to his left, placing her purse in her lap.

"Call me Shawnn," he stated.

"Okay," she conceded tersely.

As he took his seat behind his desk, he took note of the fact that she didn't allow him to be on an informal basis with her by offering for him to call her by her first name.

*Stuck up bourgeois bitch*, he thought, but kept yet another very unprofessional opinion to himself. He did this to everyone—not call them stuck up bourgeois bitches—but reading and analyzing their body language in conjunction with other subtle or subconscious signals and gestures. This was because what people unconsciously did portrayed more accurately their intentions than what they spoke verbally.

He was vigilant and good at reading people. He majored in psychology in college at one time. Furthermore, he had more than a lifetime of experience. He may have not been a certified expert, but surely enough he could read those signals as easily as he had read *The Atlanta Journal* that morning.

Shawnn noticed as she fidgeted in her chair and shied away from the sun. It was normal because it was a bright day but damn, was it that bright? He noticed that she still hadn't removed her sunhat.

He finally asked her what he could do for her. She sighed audibly going off into what seemed to be a practiced monologue.

"It's my husband," she paused before continuing once Shawnn raised his eyebrows questioningly. "I'm afraid I can't please him like I use to and there are signs pointing to his infidelity."

*I'm sure you can't, but that's T.M.I.* Shawnn thought.

She sat up perfectly in her chair, but her knee jumped up and down nervously as she patted her foot against the carpeted floor. Shawnn knew this because he could feel the quick, light vibrations, even through his heavily cushioned chair. The woman gave off conflicting signs. One sign said she was worried and concerned about something. The other portrayed her indifference to the entire situation due to her complete control; the latter of which Shawnn believed to be true.

He analyzed this simultaneously as he asked her, "Like what?"

As if on cue she went on, "He's been staying late at work a lot more lately. And when he comes home, he sometimes smells of women's perfume—not mine I mind you. Then when I call his job on the nights he says that he's working late, the secretary tells me he left hours ago."

*Wonder why?* he wanted to ask.

She had stopped momentarily to give a fake sniffle. Shawnn thought to ask her if she would like a tissue, but he didn't want to encourage this pure and utter bullshit. Furthermore, the false display of concern would have made them both phonies.

She continued, "When I brought it to his attention, he told me not to worry as long as he came home to me every night."

*Funny, I wouldn't want to come home to it either,* but instead of saying so, he asked her, "Well, what does he look like?"

On cue once again, it was show time as she reached into her purse and produced a small photograph that looked to have been taken from an identification badge. She handed it across the desk to him.

*Wow!* Shawnn didn't know what to expect but he hadn't been prepared for what was before him.

The man in the photo looked to be over three hundred pounds easy. He had huge puffy jowls, which made him look like a chipmunk with a mouth full of acorns. He had small beady eyes the color of used charcoal, with thick Poindexter glasses magnifying his atrocities. The man had no neck, but what he lacked there, he made up for three-fold with the chins he had. And this man had the gall to cheat! What could she (or he) possibly look like?

Mrs. Hamilton went on to explain how her husband—the man of many necks—worked at Trinity Enterprises. He worked every weekday 9-5:00 P.M., always taking his short breaks at the Steak 'n Shake a couple of blocks from his job.

*I can tell.* "What would you like me to do?" Shawnn wanted to know. *Besides lipo?* he thought. Tiring of her tirade and handing her back the offending picture, Shawnn was ready to get down to business. Unfaithful husbands' wives seeking incriminating pictures to receive more favorable divorce settlements was a common assignment—and easy enough to complete. But, this was not what she of the false tears had in mind. Nor did she take back the offered photograph.

With no thought whatsoever, Mrs. Triple-chin replied, "Follow him. If he's cheating, I want to know with whom and everything about her. Where she works, where she lives, how much time they're spending and a detailed physical description so that I can confront her." She said all of this with deep vindication in her voice.

"To follow a person or possibly two people my rate is—"

Shawnn was cut-off by Mrs. Hamilton saying, "I'm willing to pay five hundred a day with a five hundred dollar bonus for starting today." As she said this, she pulled a checkbook and designer pen from her purse. Scribbling quickly on it and then tearing off a check, she stood and reached across the desk to hand it to him.

"Here's three thousand to get you started. I will call you throughout the week for progress reports and will be by later this week for an update and to pay you more if it's needed." All of this came out in a rush as if uplifting a heavy burden. Finished with the terms of her agreement, she asked, "Do we have a deal?"

Shawnn was reluctant to take the job because of the bad vibes he was receiving from the woman. Furthermore, he was vexed at how she had just handled him. It wasn't like he needed the money. Business was slow, but it was damn good. He paid Jasmine better than most Fortune 500 companies paid their secretaries—though theirs probably didn't cook a mean fajita. Also, he had been investing wisely in stocks, mutual funds and real estate for years. So he was sitting on a very comfortable nest egg that was clucking well past six figures.

He thought all of this quickly but in the end came to the conclusion of *fuck it*. He couldn't see himself turning down any money, especially not for a job as easy as this would be. However, 'All money ain't good money,' he would soon find out.

Shawnn replied, "Yes," as he stood up placing the picture on his desk next to *The Times*. He accepted the check from her and sat it on his desk next to the picture. He then reached out to shake her hand and seal the deal.

When her arm shot out to comply, he was confused as she reached past him and picked a piece of his notepad stationery off of his desk. She scribbled something onto the paper and then placed it into Shawnn's still outstretched hand.

"That's my cell phone number. Call if, or when anything develops." With that she put the gold-plated blue fountain-tipped pen back into her purse.

Shawnn glanced at the paper. It had a phone number and the address to Trinity Enterprises on it. Also, 'works 9-5; lunch @ Steak 'n Shake @ 12' was scrawled on the stationery.

"I'll have my secretary draw you up a receipt before you go," Shawnn said still staring at the paper. By now she had put her checkbook back into the purse and draped it over her skeletal shoulder.

She turned to leave, but before she reached the door, Shawnn had called out to her, "Mrs. Hamilton." She turned around, eyebrows raised while still looking at the paper. He felt somewhat foolish now because there was nothing else he needed to know. He realized the name 'Harold Hamilton' was printed on the paper.

Not one to be shamed, Shawnn glanced around his desk and noted *The Times* crossword section was still visible.

"Do you happen to know a nine-letter word for 'misrepresentation'?" It was a clue he'd been boggled by earlier.

Mrs. Hamilton placed the tip of her right index finger on her thin lower lip and tapped it lightly. After a moment, she began counting off numbers from her closed fists until all but one pinky was extended. Then, without an iota of irony, she replied, "Deception."

# VI

## 2 - 11

Homicide Detective Sergeant Danny Wright climbed behind the wheel of the white 2002 Crown Victoria he had bought at the police impound auction a few years earlier. Though it was his personal car it labeled him as law enforcement at once upon inspection. The two large bandwidth antennas on the trunk helped with this assessment. Had he wanted to be inconspicuous he would have a hard time. The wire-mesh grill separating the vehicles rear seats from the front also identified him.

But if it kept him spotlighted it also helped him in traffic. His partner Thomas wondered why didn't he 'get something a little less 5-0', but he said 'it ran and got him from a-to-b'. That was the point wasn't it? He was not the flashy type. From his car to his clothes to his duplex, the man's whole style screamed mediocre. It reeked of blandness. But he was okay with that. At least he thought he was.

He cruised down Main Street despite his partner's admonishment to hurry. Wright had the windows down to let in the fresh southern air. Unlike in New York, you can breathe here. And you see the sky without it being obscured by monumental sky scrapers.

The radio was on, but the volume was low to allow the police scanner to be heard over the smooth soft-rock he was listening to.

Eight minutes and three songs after his departure, Wright saw the chaos on Broad Street in the distance. Another hectic day this will be.

He pulled up onto a curb outside of the caution tape that surrounded the filled-to-capacity lot. Wright got out of his unmarked cruiser and headed towards the eye of the storm.

Police black-and-whites were everywhere. Their flashing lights were competing with the beacon lights of the ambulances from Grady Memorial Hospital. But by far the biggest show came from the SWAT team vehicles. There were two large UPS-type delivery trucks painted black with 'SWAT' in big white block letters on the side, along with a utility van adorned the same way.

Also in the mix were the many news vans easily identified by their logos and the large satellite dishes on their roofs. News channel 9, 10, 12 and Fox were present and accounted for.

Wright walked up to the tape that had cordoned off the area. As he was about to duck under it, a beat-cop in a dark navy-blue uniform interrupted him. Wright was relieved when the officer recognized him. He didn't take kindly to the idea of having to flash his badge to get respect.

Wright couldn't remember the young officer's name off top, but upon catching a quick peek at his name plate, he asked, "How's it going Brewer?"

The officer holding up the tape line to allow Wright to duck under it replied, "It's a war zone. The media are having a field day. Someone must have tipped them off because they were here before the call came in."

They were headed towards the recently robbed Bank of America.

Wright asked Brewer, "Have you seen Captain Drafts?" referring to his squad captain who his partner said wanted to see him. This was big because normally any orders from high up in the legislative department were passed on judicially. Translation: Wright rarely spoke to the captain. Usually his orders were given to him by his supervisor Lieutenant Crump, who may or may not have gotten them from the captain, who sometimes reported to the mayor.

"He should be around here somewhere. Just look for the rising steam." Just as Brewer said this, Captain Drafts came into view looking none too happy. And there may have been a hint of steam rising from his ears.

Captain Drafts was a stout man who had lived beyond his glory years. He was 5'8, but the two hundred and thirty pounds he carried made him seem taller. He had a salt-and-pepper box haircut, typical of most military personnel. His skin was the weathered brown of a paper bag with a large bull neck. Captain Drafts' face may have been handsome had he lost around fifty pounds. His suit clung to his body as if straining to hold on. He had an angry demeanor like he was always mad at something. Today was no different, apparent from his scold.

"What took you so long Wright?" The man didn't realize that people could hear him just fine so he habitually shouted.

"I got here as fast as I could." Wright was surprised he even knew his name. In a precinct with upwards of eighty detectives, DeKalb County was one of the larger units in the peach state of Georgia. Wright figured he remembered his name from the many reprimands he'd received. Or maybe it was the few awards for tough cracked cases. Wright, as well as his partner Thomas' records did indeed precede them.

"Well, that wasn't fast enough," Captain Drafts bellowed.

"What happened?" Wright asked for an explanation, only to have his question redirected for the second time.

"Where's Detective Thomas?" the captain queried.

"I don't know. I just got here," Wright responded, indifferent to his partner's whereabouts.

"Well find your partner. Thomas has the scoop and knows everything that I want done from the short briefing we had. I don't feel like explaining the situation again. Had you been here from the start you'd already be looped in. What are you waiting for?"

For a normal man this would have been a brief exchanging of words. But coming from the raging bull that Captain Drafts is, it sounded like a heated argument. Furthermore, from the short encounters Wright had—had with the aging speaker-box, he knew he was a man of few words—other than orders. So this breathy reprimand put Wright on edge and gave him the impression that something more was amiss than a regular '2-11'.

Captain Drafts lurched off in the direction of one of the SWAT trucks. Between the hosts of different uniforms and reporters, Wright saw two detectives he had worked with. He headed to them to get answers and to see if they could help locate his partner. The two detectives were standing up under the pavilion of the Bank of America. One was half a foot taller than the other but both were white. They both had a Styrofoam cup in their hands, presumably filled with coffee.

"Kimbrell, West," Wright acknowledged the men with a head nod.

"Well if it isn't the man of the hour," West, the shorter of the two said. Wright and West had been partners in the Special Victims Unit, but Wright requested a change once he had seen that the man's scruples weren't up to par. To be precise, Wright didn't agree with evidence and crime scene tampering. Wright hadn't reported the infraction but when he requested a change of partners, he hinted that West was not 'politically correct'. Ever since then, West had been labeled a borderline racist by his peers. However, his new partner Kimbrell, who was reported to have taken bribes from a few members of the Aryan Brotherhood, didn't mind one bit. Go figure. Although they were far from friends, professional courtesy kept him and Wright on speaking terms.

"What's going on here?" Wright asked the two.

Kimbrell was the one who answered, "You haven't been briefed?"

"Obviously not if I don't know what happened," replied Wright sardonically.

"Still a late riser," stated West. Wright was tired of people talking about his sleep schedule. Protocol dictates that he could come into the office when he pleased. Just because he only needed six hours to do what took most detectives ten didn't mean he was ineffective or any less of an investigator. Results were the common goal of the division and he got those in spades.

"Yeah, whatever. Just give me a run-down," Wright intoned.

"Where's your partner? I know Thomas will have been briefed," West said.

"Yeah, that ice-box knows everything," Kimbrell replied.

Wright, tired of being diverted back to his partner stated, "We're partners not butt-cheeks. We aren't connected all the time."

"I bet you wish you were," from Kimbrell.

"Yeah, because from the looks of it, that thing has a real sweet—" Wright's intense glare cut short whatever West was going to say next. Not only was the man an in-the-closet racist, but he was sexist too.

Before Wright could voice his not so flattering opinion, Kimbrell drew his attention, "Well speak of the devil." He was looking over Wright's shoulder, so Wright turned around in that direction.

Wright saw the gathered crowd of spectators lining the caution tape. He also saw reporters interviewing people and attempting to interview police officers and detectives alike. He now made out a few FBI agents by their no nonsense demeanor. Feebs. But he didn't see. . . Wow, he couldn't believe it—though he had every reason in the world to.

Through the throng of people, he noticed a petite lean body step through unrestrictedly under the police tape. It was the most beautiful face he had ever seen in reality—and fantasy. It was the face of the woman he had been dreaming about not even thirty minutes ago.

She wore a navy-blue, creased pants suit that did nothing to hide her sensuous curves. Her low heels were businesslike, nevertheless still provocative. Under her jacket concealing two very perky breasts was a white blouse. Also, there was the tell-tale bulge of a gun in her shoulder holster.

Wright appraised her as she walked in the three detectives' direction.

She held two large white boxes in her left arm. In her right hand she had a brown lidded cup. As she drew closer Wright realized that as in his dream, she wore no make-up. Her skin was the perfect shade of butterscotch. Her hair was not down as it had been though. It was high on her head in a business bun.

Her Chanel #5 perfume could now be smelled, assaulting his nose with wanton. Finally drawing up to the men, her eyes sparkled and her lips looked to be in need of a good kissing. The woman held out the cup of coffee to Wright and then in the same sultry voice that had begged him to cum in his dream, she said "It's about time." Unlike in the dream, this was no sexual goddess. This was a homicide detective. A co-worker. His partner; Detective Veronica Thomas.

Wright accepted the coffee with a thank you. Thomas opened the top box to him and the other men saying, "I bought doughnuts. I know you haven't eaten." They each accepted one—in the case of Kimbrell, three—of the hot Krispy Kremes. Though it was stereotypical for cops to eat doughnuts, that still didn't stop them from being a quick, much needed energy boost. And Wright's favorite. She bought two boxes.

He bit into the glazed pastry with vigor because she was right, he hadn't eaten. Upon the second bite, it was gone. As he washed it down with coffee that was exactly how he liked it, he heard West saying, "How Martha Stewart of you." Wright didn't choke; barely.

"And how little dick of you to notice. . .Bartholomew," she retorted. West's blush was hard to conceal, though he tried to hide it by putting the doughnut in his mouth.

"Bartholomew?" Kimbrell mumbled around a mouth full of pastry.

Before anything else could be revealed, Thomas told Wright, "We need to talk in private. Let's go and check if the hostages have been released." With that, they turned and walked towards the direction of one of the SWAT trucks. Wright could feel the gaze of the two detectives on their backs. Well his back, her plump rear.

At that moment, Thomas turned and said, "Bye Kimbrell, see you. . . Bart." It must have been the right thing because they both looked away embarrassed.

Wright scarfed down three more of the glazed confections while Thomas daintily ate two and told him the facts. "I'm sure you talked to Captain Drafts by now," Wright was nodding between bites and sips of coffee. "So you know what's going on."

"No, he told me you'd inform me of the situation," he interjected.

"Get up earlier and maybe you'd be informed," she countered. He didn't respond so she continued. "At approximately 7:06 this morning, three men entered the bank presumed to be painters by their attire. They produced automatic weapons and placed a bomb on the center partition, threatening to blow the building up if they didn't get the money. Going against all policies and procedures, the bank tellers complied."

"Why?" Wright asked. "They could have hit the fail-safe switch and police would have been here in less than two minutes."

"We don't know yet. We're attempting to find out. Apparently the hostages thought that the incendiary device was wired to the entrance. We're waiting for their releases now."

"How did you find out if they never alerted the police?" Wright asked.

"There was an anonymous tip. Unfortunately this anonymous person tipped the media first."

"What does this have to do with us? As I said before and just confirmed a few minutes ago when I read the logo on the front doors, this bank is FDIC insured. That means it's the Fucking Blithering Idiot's jurisdiction."

As far as judicial disputes, the FBI takes precedents over all other agencies. As a result, there's latent hostility between the agencies and regional friction amongst them. There is a long standing reluctance to work together, because they compete for the glory of solving the big cases and each refuses to share the shine. Theirs was a love-hate relationship because information had to be collectively dispersed. It wasn't done freely, and the resentment continued to smolder.

"Yes, you're right. However due to the severity of the epic events upon us, and nature of the menacing methodical methods (say that five times fast) of the suspects, the FBI is requesting DeKalb County's help in apprehending these criminals." She paused for dramatic effect, then, "And Captain Drafts labeled you the lead detective this morning while you were sleeping."

Some cases will either make or break your career. This was one of them.

"He gave you free reign and control of the investigation, either to make you a hero or have you buried alive. Also, all detectives are at your disposal as of—" she paused to look at her watch. It read 7:52. "Forty-two minutes ago."

Wright thought for a moment and then said, "You knew this when you called."

It was a statement of known fact, nevertheless Thomas still answered anyhow. "Yes."

That explained why Kimbrell and West were more standoffish than usual. And why the captain didn't want to explain. He didn't like relinquishing power, hence his reluctance to admit that Wright was one of, if not the best detectives in the precinct.

Power!

"So that means you have to do everything I tell you?" This was said with a devilish glint in his eyes and grin on his face.

"There's not a paycheck big enough in this world or the next for that," Thomas said squandering the reminiscing of his dream.

"Get your mind out of the gutter," he said to her, but more to himself.

"I was about to tell you that," she responded shaking her head.

They sometimes flirted, but Wright always wondered why his advances fell on deaf ears. Neither of them were married or divorced, nor did they have any kids. To his knowledge, which was limited, she was single. Yet every time he asked her out jokingly, he was shut down. Albeit ever so gently. Maybe he needed to stop joking.

By now they had reached the SWAT van and had been standing beside it talking. The doughnuts of the first box along with the coffee were devoured and Thomas had thrown the empty box in a nearby trash receptacle in the parking lot. The plethora of spectators had grown in size and the camera crews seemed anxious for action. Or blood.

Thomas tapped on the rear panel double doors of the back of the truck. It opened to show a host of technical equipment; computer monitors, thermal imaging hardware and ionic scanners. Along with various tactical gear; flash grenades, M-16 assault rifles and coils of bungee cord.

Seated by a monitor was a man in black riot gear with a playstation-like remote control in his hands. Holding open the door to the truck was a tall man introduced to Wright as Speck.

"Good to meet you," Speck said shaking Wright's hand. To Thomas he said, "What took you so long." She handed him the other box of doughnuts. "Oh. What a godsend you are." He complimented her, taking the box and handing it to the unintroduced man at the computer. He graciously accepted it, immediately beginning to work on it.

Thomas speaking to Speck, said "Please update my partner."

Sounding as if he would have rather gorged on a Krispy Kreme first, Speck started explaining. "Once we got tipped off, we called the bank and spoke with the manager. One. . ." Speck reached behind him and grabbed a piece of paper off of one of the consoles holding up the bank of monitors. He produced a pair of large thick glasses. Placing them on his face, Wright could now see why he was referred to as Speck. As in spectacles.

Speck continued, now reading from the paper. "A Mr. Bobby Ray. Though reluctantly, he informed us that he didn't have a key to the rear dock doors on hand. Only the supervisor in charge of the Wells Fargo deliveries had that access, and he didn't come in until 11:00."

Wright spoke up asking, "So were the fire exits wired to this bomb?"

"Good question," stated Speck. "But no. The reason the manager didn't use them was because he said he was afraid the sirens would set off the incendiary device."

Wright thought that scaring your victim into inaction was a highly effective tactic.

"The supervisor was called in arriving here a few minutes ago. The FBI's HRT" (Hostage Rescue Team) "went in to release the hostages, while the SWAT" (Special Weapons and Tactics) "team secured the perimeter. If everything goes as planned they should be out any second."

As if by word of mouth, as soon as Speck spoke that last sentence, a cheer arose from the crowd of spectators. Wright, Thomas and Speck turned to find out what had caused this uproar.

From behind the bank an entourage of civilians came, followed closely and surrounded by agents in FBI wind breakers and SWAT team members in tactical gear. Wright and Thomas approached the lead agent who appeared to be in charge.

Reluctantly pulling out his badge Wright introduced them, "I'm Robbery/Homicide Detective Sergeant Danny Wright and this is my partner Detective Thomas. We will be leading the investigation for DeKalb County and I want you to know we will aid you in any way we can."

They shook hands. As the man started talking Wright flashed his badge only to have it nodded away. "No need," he stated. "I know who you are. During the wait for the bank supervisor I did a quick background check on you. Your credentials are exceptional. So are your write-ups," he smiled. "I'm Hostage Negotiator/Special Agent Brandon Levin."

Wright had always wondered if they got a promotion, would they then become "super"-special agents?

"I assume you are up to date with the crisis?" Wright nodded. "Well how may I and my agency be of assistance to you?" Levin said this with more sincerity than Wright thought possible. Levin was a short man of about 5'7. He had short cropped red hair looking to be in his early forties. His proposal threw Wright for a loop because he didn't expect the Bureau to be this cooperative.

Wright responded, "Well, first I'd like to see the scene of the crime—" He stopped short when he saw Levin shaking his head.

"That will be awhile. Right now, SWAT is sending in a rover to disable the bomb and neutralize any other threats. However, as soon as it's possible you will have access to it." A rover was the FBI's custom robot designed to sniff out and analyze any incendiary devices. If possible, the small mobile robot disabled any threats without much risk of civilian casualties. It was about three feet tall and resembled R2D2 from the

*Star Wars* movies with added prehensile extendable arms. A multitude of cameras were mounted on it giving its operator a 360 degree view of the hostile area.

Wright realized this was what the man in the van was operating with the controller. Wright continued with his requests, "Well, then I would like to be the first to review the surveillance videos—."

Interrupting again Levin said, "We will review them first and a copy will be delivered to you asap." Two for two in being given the runaround. Will he bat .1000?

"Well then, at least I can interview the hostages?" By now they were seated at the curb with medical personnel who were handing out blankets and administering minor treatment for shock. Media Relations were keeping reporters at bay—for the moment at least—while the agents were talking to the victims who weren't so shaken.

"That can be arranged," Levin said after a moment of reflection.

Before he walked up to the seated victims—no longer hostages—Levin said, "It will be easier if we split up and compare notes afterwards." With that said, he approached a young brunet with a cup of coffee clutched tightly in both hands.

Thomas said, "At least he let us do this. Are you going to ask him when you need to use the restroom too?" Before he could reply, she had chosen an older black gentleman who seemed well composed.

Wright chose an attractive white blond who looked to be in her mid to late thirties. She had a blanket over her shoulders and sat with a vacant expression in her bright green eyes.

He produced a pen and notepad from his pocket then sat next to her because he knew it would make her more at ease. He had a position of power, towering over her would make her even more uncomfortable. "I'm Detective Wright with the Robbery/Homicide division of DeKalb County. Do you mind if I ask you a few questions about what went on in there?" he implored.

Startled from her blank stare, she stammered, "I—I—I suppose."

"What's your name?" Wright inquired.

"Tammy. Tammy Sherrill. With two *r*'s, and *l*'s," she replied as Wright wrote it down.

"How old are you?" She paused showing reluctance to answer. "It's just for verification purposes."

"Fifty-two."

*A great looking fifty-two,* thought Wright. *She should be proud.* "Why were you in the bank today?"

"I work there," she explained.

"For how long?"

"Since 2008. My husband lost his job at the start of the recession and we needed the extra income," was her response.

"What do you do?"

"I'm a teller," she answered as if it should have been obvious.

"What happened today Mrs. Sherrill?"

"Miss," she corrected. "We're divorced." She sounded bitter.

"Sorry," Wright apologized.

"It's okay. I'd been miserable for a while," she had a blank expression on her face for a moment until Wright cleared his throat bringing her back. "Oh, where was I? The day started out normal. I was servicing. . ." she looked around a second before pointing, "That man over there. He was depositing a check. That's when the three men came in. We have been remodeling, so when I saw the painters I just assumed there had been a scheduling conflict. That's when the short one started to tell us about the bomb and how he was prepared to die if he didn't get the money."

"What did they look like?" Wright was hoping—in vain—for a good description.

"They had painter's coveralls covering their whole bodies. With the caps, dust masks and goggles I couldn't see much. If they were in the crowd right now I wouldn't recognize them."

*Damn,* Wright thought.

"But I'm sure they were black," she threw him a bone.

Well that narrows it down to about twelve percent of the total US population. What's that, around forty million suspects?

"If you heard them again, would you recognize their voices?"

"Only one spoke, but I would."

"So you were forced to put the money in. . ." he left it open for her to finish.

"Duffle bags. Yes. One of the taller ones held the bag while I emptied my drop box."

"Is that standard procedure?" Wright asked, knowing that it wasn't.

"See that's the funny thing. No, I didn't go by policy," she reflected.

"Why is that funny? Did you feel threatened?"

"That's not exactly it. The man who spoke for them did so with such conviction. I. . . I just felt as if I couldn't betray him. He acted as if the money was owed and belonged to him. And he had us feeling the same way. He made it logical to comply. He gave us something to think about." She had that distant look on her lovely face once again.

"What was that?" Wright asked, wondering how under a death threat this woman could speak as if the criminal wasn't what he was. . .a criminal!

"Our mortality. Our lives and the way we live them. How other people lived theirs. He made it sound like a crime to be wealthy. And giving up this money that didn't belong to us could purge us of our sins. He made us realize that each day was precious because it could be our last. Though no one spoke until the police rescued us, I could feel it. Today we will begin living our lives as if a bomb could blow us away any second."

Wow, this criminal was more than an average criminal. He was a criminal motivator. To make this suburban woman give up what he wanted, he not only played on her physical fear, he played upon her psychological fear. Smart, yet not smart enough. Or maybe she was just an inside accomplice. Only one way to find out.

"What should you have done?" Wright asked.

"Huh?" she replied perplexed.

"What is the procedure during a robbery?"

Quoting as if from a policy manual she stated, "While grabbing the currency from the shelf with your left hand adjust the stack with your right hand and discreetly press the panic button. If assailant is in direct view of shelf, conceal tracer wrap within the bills. If you're asked to remove wraps, place the marked stack of hundred dollar bills in the bundle of soon to be proffered currency."

"And you did none of these things because you felt guilty?" Wright asked with a note of suspicion in his voice.

"Not guilty, just conflicted. I'm not the only one. There were three other tellers and two managers who did not go by policy either! Why didn't they?" she said in her own defense. Being a detective over ten years Wright knew that suspicion was like a river. The only way to avoid it was to direct it elsewhere. Before Wright could continue to badger the victim, he heard an infuriated scream. Turning in the direction that it had come from, he saw that it was Captain Drafts. He looked happy earlier compared to the enraged look on his face now.

"We'll continue this later. Thank you for your time," Wright said to Ms. Sherrill before heading in the direction of the furious looking captain.

In route, Thomas caught up to him and asked, "What do you think this is about?"

"I don't know, but from the looks of it, it can't be good news," said Wright. "Where is Lenin?" he asked next.

"I haven't seen him since an agent pulled him away from interviewing that young girl a few minutes ago," she replied. Wondering if that was one of the *super*-special agents, Wright glanced at his watch. He saw that it was a quarter till nine. He had been talking to Ms. Sherrill over thirty minutes. Reaching the captain who had been standing next to the SWAT truck where earlier they conversed with Speck, Wright saw Special Agent Lenin headed to a white Lincoln Towncar.

"What's the problem Captain Drafts?" Wright asked.

"I can't believe this shit. We'll look like fucking clowns on the news tonight when the FBI releases their statement. You better solve this thing Wright! We are already catching hell over the killing of that college student."

He was referring to the accidental shooting and killing of a possible murder suspect a few weeks back. He was considered armed and dangerous, so when the police went to apprehend him and he reached into his pocket producing a small black object, the police assumed the worst. 'Fifteen shots fired' later, the man's dying words were, "I was calling my lawyer." He held a cellular phone in his quickly cooling hand. Incidents such as this and others where police had used 'excessive force' caused the media to give DeKalb County along with its officers of the law 'Hell'—as Captain Drafts put it.

"What are you talking about? What's going on?" Thomas asked, voicing Wright's exact thoughts.

"What's going on? What's going on?!" Captain Drafts ranted.

Good to know he was paying attention.

"I'll tell you what's going on! An executive branch of the Bank of America in my jurisdiction was robbed with, with. . .YOU WON'T BELIEVE WHAT!"

Wright thought, *A stop watch and a dumb-bell*, before asking, "What?" He knew that the captain wished to be prompted before revealing the astonishing news.

"A fucking brick and an egg-timer!"

*I was close*, Wright inwardly commended himself. He was starting to admire the criminal's mind and methods. He was smarter than Wright had given him credit. Just then, a uniformed officer walked up to them. Upon begging their pardon he whispered something into Captain Draft's ear.

"Great," Captain Drafts exhaled defeated. "Just great." The beat cop walked off in the direction of the spectators, no doubt to return to crowd control. After he was out of earshot, Captain Drafts said, "Not only was the bomb a phony, but so were the guns. I was informed that forensics while preparing the discarded weapons for prints, realized they were no more than plastic stage props."

Captain Drafts paused to organize his thoughts before continuing. "The rover went in and didn't detect any explosives. Upon dissecting a small piece of the bucket that housed the bomb, the SWAT guys found a brick and ticking egg-timer. Because there was no civic threat or WMD's used, the Federal Bureau is washing its hands of this investigation; leaving us to the wolves to fend for ourselves. And they do look hungry," he finished gesturing towards the media circus.

Wright heard this but was distracted. These criminals were more than smart. They were ingenious. They robbed a bank using pure force of mind and implied threats that now have been discredited; thus making the force look impotent, while the victims appear less like victims. How can they be victims if they were never in any danger? Furthermore, Wright was willing to bet that they were the ones to tip the press off. This action guaranteed to show the public that there were no casualties or any real dangers to the not-so-much-so victims or hostages. They would now just be unfortunate people. Genius.

"What is it Wright?" Captain Drafts said to Wright's vacant stare.

"Nothing, just thinking," he replied coming back to his senses.

"Well, I sure hope you're thinking about this investigation and catching these perpetrators. Because if your partner didn't inform you—you still have the lead. And that puts all eyes on you now that the Bureau is out of the foray," Captain Drafts warned, announcing his fall-guy and sacrificial lamb. Wright heard this, but his mind was still far away. He was reflecting on how Ms. Sherrill, the bank teller, glorified the robbers. Regrettably, Wright found himself admiring their presumptuousness as well. How could you not give credit where credit was due?

They were smart, but Wright considered himself smarter. He had an intimate understanding of the criminal mind. That's what made him a good detective. That's what allowed him to praise their handy work. They had won the battle, but this was a war. And Wright planned on winning that. By any means necessary. A smile spread across his face, his first of the day. Wright was beginning to formulate a plan.

# VII
## BARSTOOL BALANCE

AFTER RESEARCHING HIS QUARRY, ALONG WITH THE PERSON WHO HAD HIRED HIM, Shawnn knew little more than he had known two hours ago. Mrs. Hamilton's story appeared to check out. He had found a copy of their wedding announcement from 2005. When he saw the picture on the internet he thought they looked. . .miserable.

He had given Jasmine Mrs. Hamilton's check and told her to deposit it into the bank. Shawnn nodded to her, she was engrossed in something on her computer screen. He exited the building and walked around back to the rear near-abandoned parking lot. It was 11:40, and most of the people working for the area businesses had left for lunch.

Shawnn had everything he needed and was prepared for his lunch/stake-out. He glanced around and spotted Jasmine's late model hunter green Honda Accord. A couple of spaces next to it he found what he sought. His black 2005 Ford Taurus.

Sometimes Jasmine moved or washed the car over the weekend and from the looks of it, she had done both. He always left his car at work—because it was his 'work car'—opting to walk except for when it rained. But Jasmine never took advantage of this to his knowledge. However having her own set of keys, she could if she chose to.

Bemused, Shawnn unlocked the door and got into the interior. It was warmed from the noon sun's slight baking. The interior smelled of pine, no doubt from the green tree air freshener hanging from the rearview mirror.

Shawnn started the Ford up easily and adjusted the radio to V-103. Next, he headed up 13th Street to Steak 'n Shake.

A few minutes later he arrived at the crowded eatery. He situated himself in a booth facing the counter. This was not one of his favorite restaurants, but he enjoyed their greasy food and delectable desserts.

When the flirty waitress arrived he ordered a hamburger platter with a Coke. Minutes later his meal arrived, served with a beaming smile from the woman whose name tag read: Tameeka.

Shawnn ate at his leisure. He skimmed the newspaper he had brought to conceal his intentions and make him less conspicuous in the same leisurely fashion. He was almost finished with his meal when he caught his target in his peripheral vision coming through the entrance.

Mr. Hamilton was now balding—he had on a toupee in the picture Shawnn had in his pocket—with less hair on the crown of his head than the Mojave Desert had trees. He had a wiry beard, with short pants on that fully prepared him for a Katrina-like flood. The picture Shawnn had did Mr. Hamilton much justice.

Shawnn reached into his pocket and retrieved the small trigger to the American flag pin on the lapel of his collar. The pin concealed a tiny hidden camera. He lowered the newspaper making sure that the hidden camera was aimed correctly with an unrestricted view. Shawnn snapped two successive pictures of his target as he sat down at the bar he was facing.

Shawnn observed Mr. Hamilton a few minutes while finishing up his meal. Next, he ordered a chicken finger platter to go. Mr. Hamilton must have had the same appetite, only more voracious, because Shawnn overheard him order the same thing—times three. This made Shawnn realize that his earlier assessment of Hamilton placing him at around three hundred pounds was off by at least fifty, more likely seventy-pounds. Shawnn wondered how he was balancing his precarious bulk on the small bar stool; years of practice probably.

Giving merit to this philosophy was the fact that his three platters were now being delivered, while Shawnn was still waiting on one. Either the man had called in his order or he was such a frequent customer, he took precedence over others. His wife did say he ate there every weekday. The cook may have known what to expect when he entered.

Shawnn watched him assault the meals with no remorse. A few minutes into his attack a beautiful woman walked in. She was a much needed reprieve from watching Porky. Shawnn was entranced by this woman. He had the strangest feeling he knew her but he couldn't place her face. Furthermore, if he did indeed know her, he would not too quickly forget.

She was clothed in a sleeveless white blouse, which attempted to conceal two ample breasts that looked to be fighting for an escape from her brassiere. She wore a fuchsia knee-length skirt that hugged the contours of her hips with a thin black belt that drew attention to her slim waist. The woman had to be every bit of 5'11. Then Shawnn noticed at the base of her long legs were black high-heeled strap-up pumps exposing French-tipped toes.

Her skin was a golden bronze, reminding you of the color of honey. She had amazing lips which were moist and plump with no lipstick. Her emerald eyes sparkled, even in the restaurants dull light. Her long silky brunette hair hung straight down a couple inches below her shoulders, but not quite to the middle of her back. The woman reminded Shawnn of the actress Angelina Jolie with those lips, but he second guessed that thought as he caught a glimpse of her assets as she sat at the bar stool. Angelina Jolie had curves, but Ice T's wife Coco couldn't compete with this woman's body!

Damn!

Shawnn regained his wits and remembered his goal when he realized who she sat next to at the bar. *No, it can't be!* He snapped two successive pictures of her as he wondered what she could want with Hamilton. From his brief research, he knew the man didn't have any substantial wealth. He couldn't hear their conversation, but he could read lips well from years of practice. So that was what he began doing.

"I was starting to think you wouldn't show," said the plump man in an exhausted yet relieved voice. They began conversing between greedy bites of food.

"I wouldn't miss our meeting for the world and everything in it," confessed the woman in a placating, soothing tone.

"Would you like something to eat?" he offered with crumbs caught in his beard.

"No," declined the woman seductively. "You know what I want."

"No I don't," admitted Hamilton. "Why don't you tell me?" Insert and swallow whole chicken finger.

"Don't play coy with me—" she began, but the rest was lost to Shawnn because at that moment a man sat down on the vacant stool between them. That obscured his view of their intriguing conversation.

*Damn*, he cursed to himself while the conversing between his targets continued.

"Mr. Hamilton, I want to know who is, how and where I can find Gregory Cosby AKA 'The Great One'," she informed him in a sardonic tone. She pantomimed quotation marks in the air with her fingers as she said 'The Great One'.

"I already told you that I can't give you any information on him. Not that I have any," Hamilton replied.

"I have heard it from a reliable source that you can. So what is it going to take Harold?" She batted her eyelashes at him as she said this.

"As I told you on the phone, I—I just can't," he stammered, trying not to look at her open flirtation. She'd been working up to this point for weeks. Though this was their first meeting, she had been baiting him up on the phone with empty promises of sexual gratification, along with monetary supplement for the info she sought.

Shawnn, fed up at not being able to see or hear anymore, decided to go use the restroom and relieve himself of the three glasses of Coke he had consumed. As he passed, he caught a little speck of their ensuing conversation and discretely snapped a few more candid photographs.

The woman had her manicured hands on his. With lust in her eyes, she was begging. "Please, I'll do anything. Anything you want!"

*Wow,* Shawnn thought. *This is unbelievable,* as he entered the mens' restroom at the far corner of the restaurant. He must have unexplained or illegal income to keep a woman of her stature on the side.

Meanwhile, "Five grand," Hamilton was saying. Now it wasn't a matter of not having the knowledge, but a matter of price.

"You must be crazy," snarled the woman getting up to leave. Though she could afford it and would have gladly paid it for the information she was seeking, she didn't want to let on how desperate she was to get it. So she bluffed because she knew his type—money-hungry. If he was asking for five thousand dollars that meant he probably expected five hundred. So she would be able to talk him down with little resistance. She'd done this before.

"Two G's," he quickly adjusted while reaching out and catching her arm, which kept her from departing.

She almost reacted violently to his touch, but caught herself before doing any irreversible damage. He saw the intensity of her green eyes and released her arm.

"I'll give you one thousand dollars," she stated. It was not as a negotiation, but as a matter of fact.

"Up front," he agreed, extending the plump open palm of the hand that had just offended her.

"I'll give you half now and the other half when I receive my info," she mused digging into the clutch purse she carried. She came out with five folded one hundred dollar bills. She sat them on the countertop, ignoring and refusing to come into contact with his sweaty hand again. Once was enough for a lifetime.

Quickly she turned to leave before he could protest. "I'll call you," he directed to her back.

Over her lithe shoulder she replied, "I know," as she exited the Steak 'n Shake.

Hamilton stuffed the bills into his pocket, smearing them with grease from his fingers which had he known was there, he would have licked it off.

Harold dragged the last few French fries through the remnant of the scarlet swamp of ketchup on the soon to be spotless plate. He thought to himself, *I got twice as much as I wanted.*

Shawnn, having used the restroom, washed his hands and adjusted the hidden camera on his shirt. He caught a glimpse of Hamilton leaving the restaurant just as he was coming out of the restroom. He returned to his booth where the chicken finger platter awaited his return. It was bagged and sat on the table with the bill lying next to it.

Shawnn glanced at the receipt then produced some bills from his wallet. He laid them on the table with a generous tip. He picked up his meal and newspaper with the intentions of catching the brunette before she got too far.

As he approached the Steak 'n Shake parking lot, Shawnn peered around trying to find her with no luck whatsoever. *Damn.* But he did see Hamilton climbing into (of all the many vehicles to choose from) a red Volkswagen Beetle.

*What a cornball,* Shawnn thought approaching the Taurus.

Shawnn followed Hamilton at a large distance because he was obviously on his way back to work. A glance at his watch revealed it to be 12:23.

As Shawnn passed the Beetle pulling into the parking garage behind the large building, he looked up at the gargantuan structure. It had to be over thirty stories tall, with mirrored glass panels surrounding its concrete foundation. As imposing as any other tower gracing Atlanta's skyline, this one seemed to be a bit busier than could be explained by the noon lunch rush. This building looked deadly.

The building was Trinity Enterprises. Shawnn reluctantly snapped a picture and continued on back to Starr Private Investigators.

# VIII
# TRINITY ENTERPRISES

"Next Friday will be the unveiling banquet for the N-1000 and the plan for its use. All the sects will be present, and I'm sure overjoyed at our progress. It'll be the beginning of the end we've strived for—for so long," the stocky man said. He was of medium height, and standing in the middle of the large office of the Chief Executive Officer of Trinity Enterprises.

The man seated in the plush couch in the executive's immaculate office replied mirthlessly, "In deed. They will be amazed by our developments. The N-3 has been more successful than expected. I predict the same will be said of the 1000." He was much taller and less attractive than the other man.

"I completely agree Patrick," exclaimed the still standing man. There was a buzz coming from the inner-office intercom interrupting the two men's proud boasting.

"Yes Tennia," the standing man said leaning over the large desk centered in the office and pressing the buzzer to the machine on his right.

"A Mr. Hamilton from development is here to speak with you," informed the voice from the intercom. "He doesn't have an appointment but was very adamant that he see you at once. He says it important Mr. Montgomery."

"Send him in," the man in the custom suit she called Mr. Montgomery said depressing the buzzer.

A few moments later a sexy young secretary escorted Harold Hamilton into Cedric Montgomery's large, 30th floor office. As Tennia excused herself, Mr. Montgomery shook Hamilton's pudgy, sweaty hand.

"Thank you for seeing me on such short notice Mr. Montgomery," Hamilton said.

"No problem Mr. Hamilton. I always have time for an employee on the rise." Montgomery said this with genuine sincerity. After all, he did mean it. He knew it was good to keep an open mind for his employees for they were the heart of his business. They made it go around. Furthermore, he sometimes received invaluable tidbits of information; which he did so now.

"What is it you wanted to talk about?" Montgomery asked. The man named Patrick who was seated on the couch feigned indifference and annoyance as he appeared to ignore their conversation. But he was listening, very intently.

"The reason I needed to speak to you," Hamilton began, "was because there's a woman, a Marlana McDonald, who was very sure that I might give her information on Gregory Cosby." Patrick—if at all possible—listened harder.

Montgomery looked entertained as he asked, "Why would she think you could give this information of all people?"

Hamilton considered this before responding, "I'm not sure. We spoke on the phone a few times. She wouldn't stop pestering me until I gave her a meeting." A smoothly told lie. He sometimes called her too. He was eager for conversation, he hinted that he may know someone who knew someone, who knew what she wanted to know. More deceptive lies.

"She told me she got my number from an anonymous source who told her that I could give her info on 'The Great One.' So I relented and told her I would meet her today on my lunch break. Then I did, and I'm just now getting back and relaying the events to you." Harold finished as if a heavy burden was lifted from his chest.

Suspicious. "Why did you allow this meeting," Montgomery asked. His momentary loss of words was pause enough for Montgomery and Patrick to know what came next was a lie.

"To see what I could get out of her," was the answer without conviction.

"And what did you expect to get?" Montgomery intoned.

More shakily, Hamilton replied, "I don't know."

"Did you get what you didn't know you were looking for?" Was the set up for another lie.

"No, she didn't tell me any of what she knew." The tremor was noted in his voice.

"What makes you think she knew anything?" Montgomery implored.

Uh-oh. "I don't know," was another shaky response.

"That seems to be a popular response with you. Well, do you know that this 'Great One' is a myth? A made up phantom used to explain the classified wealth that started this company; and launched it to its successful plateau we are now comfortably seated on today." Montgomery explained this the same way he always did to people curious about the unexplainably grand start-up of Trinity Enterprises almost forty years ago in 1973. He didn't understand how anyone could believe such fictional bullshit. There was an angry glint in his eyes.

Hamilton nodded his head feebly. Patrick abruptly stood and excused himself from the well decorated office. He closed the door behind him.

Throughout this exchange, Hamilton had been standing, as was Montgomery though he was leaning against the edge of the ornate desk. He now stood completely to excuse Hamilton as he said, "Well, then there's nothing left to talk about," ending the meeting. Montgomery now had his hand extended to shake Hamilton's and escort him out.

But before Hamilton took the offered hand, he blurted out, "We have another meeting tomorrow." This was only a half lie because he did plan on meeting her after he scheduled one tonight. Not to give info, but to receive the other five hundred dollars.

*Interesting*, Montgomery thought, *I wonder why*. He considered this while Harold shifted under his scrutiny. Then Montgomery turned to the desk and hit the buzzer.

A second later, Tennia's nice voice spoke sweetly, "Yes Mr. Montgomery?"

He pressed the buzzer to reply, "Are there any openings in my schedule this week?"

After a brief pause came the response, "No sir, not until the 16th. There's a free hour from 9:00 to 10:00 A.M."

"Nothing else sooner?" Montgomery implored.

"Wait. . . yes, Mr. Jones—the representative of Smith and Wesson—cancelled earlier today because of a scheduling conflict. That leaves you an hour opening Wednesday, the 9th at 2:30," Tennia elaborated.

"Well book a Miss. . .what's her name?" he said to Hamilton.

"Who?" Hamilton replied dumbfounded.

"The curious woman you came to see me about." *Who else?*

"Mar—Marlana McDonald," he stammered. Montgomery echoed the name into the intercom.

"Alright Mr. Montgomery," Tennia said signing off.

Speaking to the pudgy man in front of him once again, Montgomery said, "When you meet Ms. McDonald—she is a Miss right?" Harold nodded, his three chins rolling with the motion. "Tell her to meet me here at 2:30 on Wednesday, and I'll give her the info she needs on 'The Great One'." Harold was afraid of this. Montgomery's tone was too ominous.

He left the office feeling numb and as if his betrayal set Marlana up for failure. Or worse, doom. He didn't know if he did right by bringing this to the CEO or not, but he knew it felt wrong. At least he had something to give her for the grand.

Meanwhile, elsewhere in the Trinity Enterprises building. . .

"Why did I just leave Cedric's office where a man, or what appeared to be a man trapped in a walrus' body, was asking about 'The Great One'?" Patrick spoke with rage lacing his voice, also a trace of fear. He asked this to the woman seated behind the desk in a large, but not as large as Cedric Montgomery's office. She was known as Toccarra.

"I told you I have everything under control," she replied. Her demeanor was always calm. And calculation could be seen in her light-gray eyes. Though she was seated, you could tell she was petite. But her voice commanded attention; if her looks did not. She had blond hair cut into a pixie-bob with honey-blond highlights. She wore eyeliner and make-up that added an artificial aura of beauty. Her lips, covered in red lipstick, were thin. Her nose was upturned at its narrow point, making it resemble a ski-slope. She had a widow's peak at the top of her small forehead. Overall, she was attractive in a common sort of way. Or a deceptive way.

"I hope you do have it under control," Patrick vented. "We've come too far to fuck-up now." He was pacing the office nervously.

"Rest assured Patrick, someone is on the case." She pressed the intercom and murmured, "Send Heather in." Several moments later, Mrs. Hamilton gracefully entered the secluded office, clad in the same dress she had worn to her appointment at Starr Private Investigators.

With no introductions or preamble of politeness, Toccarra said to her, "Inform Mr. Brewer here of your plans," referring to Patrick—Patrick Brewer.

"I've been assured that I have the best investigator in the city, possibly all of Georgia working to find this mystery woman in cahoots with my husband." Mrs. Hamilton spit the last words out as if they tasted bad. "I've been told if he couldn't find a person, they didn't exist—on earth at least."

"How long is it going to take?" asked Brewer.

"Hopefully we'll have her by the end of the week," Mrs. Hamilton replied confidently.

Toccarra said, "She's been well compensated." She turned to Hamilton and said, "Haven't you?" Mrs. Hamilton nodded as Toccara smiled revealing sparkling white teeth.

"I'm sure," responded Patrick Brewer, neither convinced, amused or impressed as he exited the secluded office.

# IX
# LOST AND FOUND

Shawnn entered his decorated office and handed his 'assecreceptionist' Jasmine Whitt the chicken fingers platter he had bought her for lunch. She was standing at the corner of her desk dropping small pellets into the tiny fish bowl that sat there. It was layered with pink rocks and contained a multicolored beta—the Chinese fighting fish.

"Thank you Mr. Starr," she beamed accepting the food. He often brought her lunch and on the days he didn't, he informed her so she could make other arrangements. Or, he manned the office while she went out. Those times were rare. So it always lifted his spirits when she still got excited about him bringing her lunch as if it were a present, instead of an everyday occurrence.

Heading to his office, Jasmine stopped Shawnn in a musical voice saying, "Don't forget your meeting at 1:30 with Mr. Clark."

He had almost done that. Reflecting on the beautiful woman who had been with Mr. Hamilton had convoluted his mind.

Well that's what he paid her for, right? "Alright Jasmine, thanks." He glanced at the wall clock, it read 1:12. Shawnn went into his office and retrieved the prepared portfolio from the black filling cabinet. It was for a man—Mr. Clark—searching for his daughter whom he had lost contact with and hadn't seen in over fifteen years.

The portfolio was concealed in a manila filling folder and contained over forty big glossy candid photographs with dates, times and addresses.

Shawnn had found the man's long lost only child. . .with no trouble at all.

# X
# NO COMMENT

"I<small>S IT TRUE THE HOSTAGES WERE NEVER IN ANY DANGER?</small>" <small>ASKED ONE REPORTER</small>, starting a barrage of questions.

"Are there any suspects?" Asked another.

"Why did Captain Drafts announce you as lead investigator?"

"Will any innocent people be shot?"

"How much money was taken?"

"Is the FBI still involved?"

"Were any of the hostages hurt?" The questions continued.

"How come…"

Fending off the media with shields of 'No Comment', Detectives Thomas and Wright made it to his unmarked Ford. After shutting the doors, starting the engine and then revving it to let the reporters blocking their escape know he wasn't playing, Wright was now cruising south down Broad Street. He peeked at the clock and saw that it was 1:13. They had been interviewing the hostages over four hours and Wright was ravenous.

After the thorough interviews, Wright had time to investigate the crime scene. He learned nothing of any significant value much to his dismay. Now, in theory, they were headed to the department to write up their reports and start the real part of an investigation; foot work.

Thomas, who had caught a ride from the station with another detective when the original 2-11 came in, was seated in the passenger seat of the Crown Victoria. She was distraught. But Wright, by now use to her moods and sensitive of them though she loathed his sympathy, asked, "What is it?"

As if waiting to be prompted, she vented her frustrations now with resolve. "This whole situation doesn't sit right. The hostages seemed destitute. They had no anger, or animosity at being held against their will—or at being threatened with death if they didn't cooperate. Furthermore," she continued as Wright drove but still gave her rapt attention. "They related to the criminals who did this; sympathized with them. I would wager if this went to trial, seventy-five percent wouldn't even testify for the state. It was like they were suffering from premature Stockholm syndrome." She finished referring to a psychological behavior that sometimes affected kidnap and hostage victims. After being captured or abducted, the victim forms a mental bond with the captor over time as a defense mechanism and way of coping with the dismal situation. This bond grows into a feeling so intense sometimes, that upon rescue, the person defends his or her captor with unrequited vigor and sometimes force. It can extend to the point where they feel as if they have a genuine love for their captors.

But this syndrome takes time alone with the captor over an extended period for it to develop to this stage. Not the two minutes that these people were with the bank robbers.

Throughout Thomas' rant, Wright had nodded his agreement. Not to placate her, but because he agreed with what she was saying and her perspective.

"I can't believe that we have nothing to go on."

Veronica Thomas was from Puerto Rico. She and her family had been in the United States since she was eleven. But at times when she was stressed, the slight accent of her heritage came out. She did not like it either. She was proud of her ancestry but now considered herself an American. Note the Prada blouses and Fendi pocketbooks. That is also why she'd had her name changed from Valencia Gomes. It didn't change her exotic looks one bit though.

They continued discussing the various interviews and their outlook on them until Wright pulled into the McDonalds drive-thru on Marietta Street. He hadn't eaten since the few doughnuts he'd had earlier.

"I want two McDoubles, two McChickens, two medium fries," — he knew the dollar menu well—"an Oreo McFlurry and a diet coke." Turning to Thomas he said, "Do you want anything?"

She always nagged him about his eating habits, just as she did about his sleep patterns. But the case must have had her feeling melancholy, because she replied, "A grilled chicken salad and a parfait." She always watched her exquisite figure.

He echoed her request into the speaker. After he paid for and received their food, they were on the way to the station. Between bites of greasy unhealthy food, Wright attempted to lighten Thomas' dark mood by asking, "Why don't I take you out to dinner tonight?"

He was kidding, but in a dead serious way.

As she nodded towards the empty burger and fry wrappers, Thomas replied with sarcasm, "You've had enough for the day."

He felt shot down in a not-so-hurtful way. This was how it had been for the past six months since the dreams started. Wright always asked her out and she always had some excuse or gently declined. It had become an ongoing joke between them. Some of their coworkers were even in on it from overhearing her turn him down so many times.

Though his reoccurring dreams kept hope alive, subconsciously, he had long since abandoned any thoughts that they would ever go out. Much less have a physical or sexual relationship.

He continued to wonder why though. To his knowledge, she was single and he didn't have any hopeful prospects knocking at his door. But it never failed that she declined his offers. On most occasions she had a lame excuse as she did now.

"I think I'll be in need of a recharge by tonight. How 'bout it?" Wright pressed with fries going in as the words came out.

"I would, but you're just not my type," was her often used excuse.

"What, I'm not sexy enough?" he asked with a smile. His cheeks were filled with fast food which caused him to resemble a chipmunk with a mouth full of nuts.

He was cute. But she valued his friendship and didn't want to complicate things. But his rugged good looks complimented his ruffled off-the-rack suit.

She smiled at his efforts and innocent sexiness.

"No, it's not that. It's just not the right time."

He'd heard that before. He seen her give him the once over as she often did, so he asked, "What, is it because I don't dress as immaculately as you? What, you don't think classy-sexy and cheap-handsome match?"

She laughed. He liked the way it sounded. After she composed herself, "It's not you, it's me."

*Dumped and we're not even together.*

Changing the subject she asked, "When are you going to get a new car? You don't get tired of people thinking you're out to bust them?"

Wright noticed her ploy to change the direction of the conversation, so he asked, "What if I had a different more luxurious car? Would I have a chance then?"

She avoided the topic again and replied, "You couldn't afford another car period—much less a *luxurious* one on this salary."

He saw her mood was more cheerful since it was off the case, so Wright dropped his futile efforts at seduction. But there was something else on his mind. "Tell me about Bartholemule." He referred to an incident earlier with another feminist detective.

"Oh, that," was her coy reply. "Well, with the guys, I get a lot of grief you know. Pussy-envy. So I keep a well-stocked arsenal of dirt at my disposal for use in situations like that one. *Bartholemule* is West's embarrassing first name that he attempts to hide on his tax returns and police reports."

"I thought his name was Eugene?" Wright intoned.

"That's his middle name," she explained.

"How did you come across that tidbit of invaluable information?"

"I keep my sources undisclosed," she protested.

"Do you have any ammo in your arsenal for me?" he wondered aloud.

"I plead the fifth," she said, then added, "It's not like your record isn't embarrassing enough as it is." They both shared a knowing smile.

By now, they had arrived at the DeKalb County Police Department—the second largest in Georgia. DeKalb County had over 700,000 citizens within a 271 square mile radius. It operates out of six area precincts. The seven story, brick building was home to over 1,500 inmates. While 1,112 sworn police officers and 498 support staff employees maintained the facility. The detectives' quarters and squad room was located on the first floor of the crowded structure.

After he pulled into and parked in the motor pool on the ground level, Thomas and Wright boarded an elevator to ascend to the first floor. Once the elevator came to a stop, it dinged and opened into the center of chaos of the busiest police force in Georgia.

They stepped off the elevator while phones rang everywhere, and the daily grind of being a police officer could be seen executed throughout the office squad room.

Thomas went to type up the reports of their unfruitful earlier endeavors in the case. She often did so and just handed Wright a copy to sign because he was computer illiterate and hated to write. Plus she was good at it and enjoyed it.

While she did that, Wright went to his cubicle—which was very small in the cramped police department—to do police work. When he reached his cubicle, he found a report on his desk that he had requested from the bank manager before he left the scene. It must have been faxed to him and another detective delivered it to his desk.

On the report, Wright first read something he had already assumed. The bank was insured up to a two million dollar loss.

But the real question was how much did they actually lose. As he read on about the stipulation to the contingency plan, Wright found what he was looking for.

Seven hundred twenty-six thousand nine hundred five dollars was stolen according to the statement. *Damn, that's a lot of McDoubles.* Wright imagined what he would do with three-quarters of a million dollars for a moment before the phone on his desk rang.

"Robbery/Homicide, this is Detective Wright," he answered.

"Where have you been? I've been trying to reach you over an hour?" the man on the other line said.

"Busy," was Wright's simple reply with no idea who he was talking to.

"Well, I'll be there in a minute with the package," replied the man. Then the guy hung up.

Wright hadn't considered what to do before he saw a tall police officer in uniform get off the elevator and navigate the maze of desks toward him.

When the man reached him, as usual, Wright recognized the face but couldn't place a name to it.

"I never thought you'd get here," said the officer as he shook Wright's hand. B. Jones was his name. Thank God for name plates.

"What do you have for me Jones?" Wright asked the officer.

"I have what you requested. The surveillance video of the robbery," Jones said as if Wright was a kindergartener. He held out the VHS tape (who still used those?) that was in a white sleeve. Wright accepted it. The best news he had gotten all day.

"I tried to deliver it to you earlier but you weren't here. So I took the liberty of reviewing the tape. Take my word for it, there's not much to go by."

*Yeah, to your untrained eyes and ears.* Wright thought to inform the beat-cop of the severity of obstruction of justice—which he surely knew. Also to inform him of the meaning of maintaining the integrity of an investigation—which he again surely knew. But he decided not to let the cop's insolence damper his high spirits.

He was rewarded for his restraint with, "And you won't believe what I found out."

*What, brushing helps to control the bad breath you seem to not realize you have?*

Instead of saying that, Wright took a cautionary step back and then waited for Jones-of-the-halitosis to continue.

"Do you know Officer Brewer who was on perimeter patrol at the scene today?" hot breath asked.

"Yea," Wright replied thinking of the officer who allowed him to enter the scene without showing ID. He wondered where this was going, and soon found out.

"Well, he pulled over a white van today and was about to run the van's plates—which would have come back stolen, but he had to abandon the routine stop because the call came in about a 2-11 at the Bank of America," Jones said excitedly as he exhaled more nausea inducing fumes into the air.

It took Wright a moment to put two and two together. "And that van is the same van I will see leaving the Bank of America after the robbery in a rush on this tape," Wright said as he tapped the tape against his flat palm. How does that make DeKalb County Police Department look?

"Well, I wouldn't say 'in a rush'," replied Jones. The *sh* sound in *rush* singed Wright's eyebrows.

Eager to dismiss this man so he could breathe again, Wright said, "Anything else?" It was a challenge, not a question.

The officer paused for a moment in thought before, "And I was asked to tell you that the bomb sensors on the doors to the bank were just common refrigerator magnets."

*Well I'll be.* "Thank you," Wright said relieved. After that, Officer Jones left to elude brushing and flossing for yet another day.

Wright took the tape to the audio/visual room on the west side of the department. It was normally used to tape depositions of people who were unable to testify and confessions of criminals. Also it was used to review undercover surveillance and exculpatory evidence. But today it wouldn't be used to corroborate criminals being at the 7-Eleven at the approximate time of the murder, giving him an alibi and get out of jail free card. Today it will be used to catch the bad guys, not set them free.

The small room was similar to a closet. It was devoid of any furniture other than a folding metal chair and the 13 inch combination TV/VCR on a rolling metal stand.

Wright plugged in the TV because some jack-ass thought unplugging it after every use would save the department money, then he inserted the tape and pressed play.

He sat on the edge of the flimsy metal chair as the screen lit up with a quad-sectioned view of the bank. Each camera gave a vivid black and white image of its section. It was 2011, and not only was the bank too cheap to go digital, it was too cheap for color.

Wright watched the video intently observing hand gestures and body language, listening to the sound and tone of voice of the man who spoke. Obviously the leader, he got a feel for his personality and the type of person he was. Wright became one with the criminal on a psychological and spiritual level. At least the bank splurged on sound.

As soon as the tape ended with the van leaving the parking lot—it was two minutes and twenty-nine seconds long—Wright rewound it and watched it again.

He formulated a plan. He smiled not only at their genius, but his too.

# XI
# RESTRICTED

When David Clark left Starr Private Investigators, he was elated and cried tears of joy. He hugged the portfolio that contained the pictures of his estranged daughter. It was clutched to his chest as if it could run away from him. Mr. Clark was pleased with Shawnn's work ethic. He praised Shawnn saying he went 'above and beyond his expectations.'

"You're welcome," was Shawnn's modest reply. After David Clark left his office beaming, Shawnn decided to extend his search parameters on his most recent target. He chose to evaluate his place of employment. Shawnn logged onto the internet and pulled up the homepage of Trinity Enterprises.

The company was an electronics device and weapons manufacturer. They owned corporate buildings in almost every major city in the U.S. Furthermore, there were manufacturing sites in places such as Sidney, Tokyo, Berlin, Sao Paulo, Beijing and Moscow. The complex in Atlanta was unique because it was one of the few containing a research and development facility, along with manufacturing capabilities.

Shawnn browsed the public access website with rapt attention. He was intrigued not by its contents, but also its configuration. There were very detailed pictures of weapons and devices Trinity manufactured and had on the market for not just public, but private agencies. The website gave detailed descriptions of the listed items and their various uses.

There was a link on the site that gave ordering information and the choice to buy online via paypal, check or major credit card. There were discounts for bulk orders and government agencies who wished to purchase weapons. Trinity Enterprises had a wide and extensive inventory.

Shawnn continued to browse and deemed some of the devices either useless and/or redundant. *What would anyone need with a machine that drew blood whole but left the plasma in the donor? Plasma is what makes the medicine*, Shawnn thought to himself. The only people who could use a device like that would be a. . . his contemplation was cut short by a knock at the door. "Come in!"

"I'm going home. I was just checking to see if you needed anything before I left," Jasmine clarified.

He glanced at his watch. It was 5:18. He must have lost track of the time while engrossed in the contents of the Trinity Enterprises website. "No, but thank you Jazz. Did you remember to clear my schedule for the rest of the week so that I may work on the Hamilton file?" Shawnn asked knowing she did.

"There were no pressing issues, so it's clear Mr. Starr," was Jasmine in a pleasant voice.

"Alright, see you tomorrow," Shawnn promised.

"Bye-bye," was said with a wave as Jasmine turned to exit his office. It took sheer willpower not to glance at her shapely derrière. She was sweet but he was her boss. She was too young for him—Way too young. And not his type.

Shawnn glanced back at the computer thinking of how much time he had lost. On the screen was a weapon referred to as the N-3. He clicked the description and properties bar and was surprised when a page popped-up saying: "Unavailable/Restricted." It went on to describe how the gun (that's what it looked like to Shawnn) had been recalled and reconfigured due to 'excess anomalies.'

*Sounds like techno bullshit*, Shawnn thought. He left the website opting to check his e-mail accounts. Other than the advertisements that the spam-blockers promised to stop, Shawnn had no new messages or responses to the question he sought an answer to.

"Where will the light lead us?"

After he powered down his computer Shawnn locked and left his office. On the street now, he turned to see the setting sun to the west. As always, it looked alive with the promise to rise again tomorrow. "Hell of a day," he said aloud. Next he proceeded up the street towards home to prepare for what he knew would be a hell of a night.

# XII
# GUCCI MANE'S GUN

THE DARK ROOM WAS ILLUMINATED BY THE BLACK AND WHITE SCREEN. THE MAN had been alone in it for so long and so intent on what he was doing, he didn't even hear the other person enter the room from the door situated behind him.

The man was so surprised and startled when he felt the hand rest on his shoulder that he almost jumped from the seat and pulled his service weapon. Wright was relieved when he realized that it was his partner Thomas.

"So this is where you've been all day?" she asked.

"What," was his confused reply.

"I was looking for you and couldn't find you," Thomas clarified.

"Uh, yeah. I've been watching the tape of the robbery."

"This whole time," she asked exasperated. "How many times have you watched it?"

"Huh?" was his dumbfounded utterance.

"What are you, punch-drunk or something?" she asked perfunctorily. "It's almost 5:30. That tape can't be any more than three minutes. They told me you've been watching it since around 1:30. That's four hours. If my math is correct, that means you have seen it upwards of eighty times."

*More like a hundred.* Wright glanced at his watch to see she was correct. It was 5:22. He must have lost track of time. He was so engrossed with familiarizing himself with his quarry.

"Why were you looking for me?" Wright asked her.

"What?" she replied.

"What are you, punch-drunk or something?" he got her back.

"Touché," she admitted defeated. "The reason I was looking for you was so that you can read over and sign this report. Then I can turn it in to Lieutenant Crump," she explained. She handed him the papers she held out.

"You've *been* forging my signature, what's stopping you now?" Wright retorted with the simple fact as he signed the appointed spaces without reading it.

"Before, you were just Detective Sergeant Wright. But now, you're Detective Sergeant Wright—head detective of the 'Hijinks Heist'," she said smiling.

"What?" Wright asked confused.

"What are you, punch-drunk and deaf?" she asked, going up one again. "Ever since the FBI released their statement, the press has deemed the event the 'Hijinks Heist!' That's because the robbers stuck up the bank with toy guns," she told him.

"When was this?" Wright wanted to know.

"While you were watching TV," she said and nodded at the screen. "The FBI liaison gave a press release at 4:00. By five, the news had appropriately dubbed the title. You would have known this had you come up for air."

"Yep, a lot about my new best friend," responded Wright.

"What," she asked confused. Seeing the look in his eyes, she discerned what was coming from his mouth next.

"What are you, punch-drunk and deaf?" she said the last part in unison with him. "Were you heading home?" he asked next.

"Yea, as soon as I turn these reports in to Crump. Unless you have something else we can do to solve this case or any bright ideas, everything else on the agenda can wait until tomorrow," Thomas said.

"I do," he replied with a devious smile.

"If it's like your last plan that almost got me fired, I don't want anything to do—."

"No, no, no. It's nothing like that," Wright reassured her. She had been referring to an incident a month or so ago. They had to catch a murder suspect who Wright assumed had been hired. But he didn't have any concrete evidence. So he proposed that Thomas pretend to be a wife who wanted her husband killed for his fortune. Though this undercover job wasn't approved or even asked about (because Wright knew it would be dismissed as reckless and without merit) Thomas consented to be the beautiful wife. Though she thought it a sexist way to go about the case, Wright cared about results. The investigation went sour when the night before the man who was to attempt the hit came on to Thomas. After being denied, he tried to use physical force to overcome her reluctance. Bad idea. Though Thomas looked soft and sweet in her beautifully packaged body, beneath that exterior lay the demeanor of a hardcore fighter. She broke the man's jaw in three places and nearly crushed his windpipe.

Though Wright took the blame and full responsibility for the blunder saving Thomas' job, she still brought the infraction up when he proposed a plan.

It helped that after the man was released from the hospital, Wright was waiting with Grand Jury indictments for 1st degree murder and conspiracy to commit murder. Thomas refused to press charges for the assault.

"All I need you to do is drop me off somewhere," Wright clarified.

"Yeah right. It always starts out with, 'all I need you to do is'," she said as she exited the audio/visual room.

As Thomas went to take Lieutenant Crump their reports, Wright located a phonebook and looked up the place he intended to go to.

Calling the business, he found out they had what he was looking for and the service he wanted. They told him he needed to hurry though, because they closed at six. It was 5:40. This was good. Wright wanted to get there just as they were closing.

He made one more quick stop in the department before meeting up with Thomas.

⌒⌒⌒

After he dropped off his 'Fix or Repair Daily' Crown Victoria, Wright was seated in the passenger seat of Thomas' 2007 maroon Cadillac STS—American enough for you? They were lost in their own thoughts letting the smooth jazz fill their silence.

As they cruised down Peachtree Street more smoothly than he ever did she announced, Wright looked out of his passenger-side window at Atlanta's deceptively beautiful infrastructure.

When they passed Atlanta's Fulton County Stadium—the home of the Braves and Falcons—Wright relived the pain of being put out of the NFC playoffs by the Green Bay Packers. The Packers also put out the Philadelphia Eagles and Atlanta's former star quarterback: Michael Vick. The Falcons finished the season in the NFC South as 13/3, clench-ing the division title and having a first round bye and home-field advan-tage in the playoffs. However, the wildcard Packers who were 10/6 won the Super Bowl. Ain't life a wildcard bitch?

Thomas pulled up to Wright's destination saying, "I still don't see why you're here or what it has to do with the Hijinks Heist."

"Do you want to know my plan?" Wright asked.

"Yes, I'm curious. As long as it won't incriminate or implicate me in any of your not-so-legal ploys," she replied. She was quoting how he described the above the law investigative tactics he sometimes implemented.

"Well over dinner, I'll explain after I'm through here. What time would you like me to pick you up?" he asked smiling.

"No thank you. I'm not *that* curious," she responded. Wright got out of the car. She rolled down the window and asked, "Are you sure you're okay?"

"Yea, I'm pretty sure," he replied.

"Well I'll see you tomorrow. Maybe you'll decide to surprise me and show up early—or ironed," she kidded, knowing it'd take nothing short of the work of God to get him to the department before 8:00.

"If we went out to dinner tonight, I could spend the night at your house afterwards and you could make sure I was up to get there early," he suggested. He was eager and willing if she accepted the offer.

"What are you, punch-drunk and deaf?" she responded smiling, and laughed as she pulled away. Wright turned and navigated the many cars to enter the lobby of CIA—Connoisseur Import Autos.

Inside, the first thing Wright noticed was the mirrored showroom floor. On it, sat a black 1928 Cadillac 341 Sport Phaeton. Wright only knew because of the large sign that hung over it and proclaimed it so. Next to it in stark contrast, was a white 1935 Mercedes-Benz 500K Special Roadster. Wright didn't have much time to evaluate these rare beauties because soon after he entered the lobby, a man approached him coming from an open office.

"And you I presume, are Aaron Jennings," said the man who extended his hand for a shake. Wright nodded at the cover name he had given him earlier. He was posing as Aaron Jennings, the personal manger of Atlanta's very own up and rising star, Radric Davis AKA Gucci Mane.

Wright knew of the manager Aaron Jennings from a personal experience with Davis when the rap artist who was not quite a star yet, was indicted for murder. Apparently, four men burst into a young woman's home that the rapper was visiting and attempted to rob him. Gunfire was exchanged and three days later a man was found dead in front of a middle school. Gucci Mane was later arrested. Jennings and Davis' attorney (Dennis Scheib) were at the station every day petitioning for the release of their client, arguing it was self-defense. Though Davis never proclaimed innocence, the charges were later dropped due to lack of evidence!

That's code for money exchanging hands under the table.

After they shook hands, the Arabian man with copper skin introduced himself, "I'm Faqui Muhammad." There was no trace of an accent whatsoever. "The owner of CIA." Wright knew who he was and about the business he conducted.

"Well buddy, let's see if we can put you in that car you wanted," said Muhammad with his dealer spiel. He led Wright out onto the lot. No one else was there which is how he wanted it.

They talked and walked to the car Wright had inquired about earlier. Muhammad said, "I was starting to think you weren't going to show-up buddy. I've sent my staff home. I was about to close."

That was also just how Wright wanted it. He was there under the guise of renting a car to be used in Gucci Mane's next music video. He looked at his watch, it was 6:10.

After they passed by many customized Ferraris, Lamborghinis and Rolls Royces, they finally arrived at the car Muhammad had insisted would be perfect for the rap star's video with singer Mariah Carey.

"This buddy," the salesman began, "Is the crème-de la crème of coupes." The car he referred to was parked helter-skelter between a gold Jaguar S-type and a black Porsche Carerra. It put both of them to shame.

"This is the 2010 Bentley Continental Supersport," Muhammad said in an excited tone as he opened the driver's side door. Wright didn't know much about cars, but he knew class when he saw it. Muhammad unlocked the passenger door from the panel. Next, he walked around to the other side and told Wright to get behind the wheel from over the hood. They both got into the car.

Wright sunk into a seat so plush, he felt as if he were floating on a cloud. Though the exterior was stark white with tiny flakes of sparkles on it, the interior was a deep red. A red the color of cranberry sauce.

Wright, hypnotized with luxury, didn't realize for a moment that Muhammad had been speaking.

"This baby is one of the fastest vehicles leaving the manufacturing line. Its 622 horses can cause her to gallop at up to 204 miles per hour. Furthermore, the engine has a flex-fuel integration system that allows it to run on E-85. The suspension is great, but even if it wasn't as you can feel, these racing bucket-seats would pick up any slack."

"This precious piece of beauty is particularly special because I have it sitting on offset Asanti Rims. Each has a seven inch lip, with twenty inches in the front and twenty-two's in the back causing this baby to pout. You want to hear her cry buddy," Muhammad asked, sticking the key into the dashboard ignition. "Start her up," he directed.

Wright did just that, and almost wished he didn't. The car came to life with a silent rumble so exotic, it seduced Wright into an instant love deeper than he had ever felt for any woman.

Muhammad was still talking, "The price tag on this one was two hundred and seventy grand. . ." He went on, explaining the different features and interior console originalities. But all of that flew right over Wright's head. He just loved the way the steering wheel felt in his pistol hardened hands.

Eventually they had to talk business, and Wright found himself in the man's spacious office, wishing he was back in the Bentley.

"Well," Muhammad began to explain while seated behind his desk. "The rate for the Continental is three grand a day. That covers insurance as well. With who you are, I'll leave the option to buy open with the accumulated daily rate deducted from the total price. I'm doing this because I'm sure once Gucci gets in her, he'll be *"In Love"* like his song says." Wright didn't know what song he was referring to, or any of Gucci Mane's songs for that matter. He detested rap music. He still smiled.

Playing his role of devil's advocate, Wright asked, "And what is the total price?"

Dollar signs flashed in Muhammad's eyes like the slot machines in Vegas. He licked his lips, and looked to have strained to refrain from rubbing his hands together. When he replied, "For you and who you represent, and because he bought that Lambo from me last year, I'll let her go for a dollar-ninety." He said a hundred and ninety thousand dollars as if it were change.

Wright didn't want the car he told himself, he only asked because he was curious and it kept up his guise. Wright couldn't see himself with that vehicle. Not out of love of his Ford, and not because he couldn't afford it, but because a car of that caliber changes people. Not just their outer appearance, but all the way to their soul. He didn't mind not having flashy suits or flashy cars. He was happy just being him. There was more to life than money and women—at least more than money.

"Well, let's just rent her for now. Then we'll see if—as you said—once he gets in her, he falls *"In Love."* Wright responded cryptically.

This satisfied Muhammad because he said, "I'll draw up the necessary paper work. How many days will you need her?"

Wright, when making his plan, hadn't considered that. Quick on his feet he responded, "The video shoot is set to run three days. But Mariah Carey is a certified diva, so who knows how long it will take." Muhammad nodded understandably. "Just leave the dates open, like the option to buy."

That brought the man's spirits up again as he began to type at the computer on his desk. "Don't worry, I'll handle the paper work. I just need your license."

Wright pulled out the quickly forged license containing Aaron Jennings class picture from his wallet for the eager salesman who then began the required documentation.

Idly, Wright pulled a fat knot of money from his pocket after he had put his wallet back in his pants. He had signed the money out of the storage locker as petty cash before he left the department. Certain expenses incurred during an investigation could sometimes be reimbursed. Or, if it's a slight charge like taking a witness to dinner, it could be covered with petty cash. But three thousand dollars a day, for who knows how long may not be covered—especially if his plan doesn't succeed.

The money in Wright's hands was far less than it appeared to be. The hundred or so one dollar bills were wrapped with ten twenties. So in all it was more like three hundred dollars, but looked like thousands.

"There's one more order of business," Wright said to Muhammad, whose eyes had grown big at the sight of the flash-cash as Wright fake counted it.

"What else can I do for you buddy?" Muhammad asked, eager to please; or to see more money.

"Radric asked me to inquire about 'automatic' imports." Wright said this with a trace of innuendo. He had just signed the rental/insurance agreement. "I wasn't talking about cars," Wright said. This was a back-up ploy Wright had devised to get the luxury car. That was the reason he chose this particular dealership out of the hundreds in Atlanta. Though he was fishing and didn't know if it was true, word was that Faqui could get you anything. From an Israeli-made Uzi sub-machine gun, to a host of RPGs (Rocket Propelled Grenade launchers).

The ATF (Bureau of Alcohol, Tobacco and Firearms) and the GBI (Georgia Bureau of Investigations) were privy to this information, but after years of covert operations, stings and illegal wire taps, they had to drop the case for lack of funds and evidence. The agencies had competed with each other for the bust vigorously. It was obvious to Wright at least, that Faqui was under surveillance. And it was obvious that he knew it too. The case and investigation had been dropped over two years ago. Just long enough to lull Faqui back into a false sense of security and let down his guard. As he did now.

"What are you talking about Mr. Jennings?" Suspicion laced his voice, and it was the first time he hadn't referred to Wright as buddy.

"Call me A.J.," Wright said all buddy-buddy now.

Abruptly Muhammad asked, "Are you the police, or a member of any law enforcement agency?"

Wright could've given him the run-around on this question but he was sure if he did, the jig was up. Muhammad was smart. He knew that as an officer of the law, if asked, they had to identify themselves. If not, any information or evidence obtained under the false pretense of not being the law could not be used against them. It would fall under rule 45 section 3(b) of the state statue: Entrapment.

With that in mind, Wright replied smoothly, "Hell no! Why would you ask that?" They'd have to prove he said it. Otherwise, it's Wright's word against his; an officer of the law versus a lowlife Arabian gun-runner. Who would you believe? We know who the judge is going to believe.

"Just had to ask. Don't want to get T.I.'d this time around," Muhammad explained. Wright nodded again, having no idea what *T.I.'d* meant. He was referring to another of Atlanta's rap star elite who was busted a few years back for buying guns from federal agents. Oh, *T.I.'d.*

"It depends on what you have on short notice. Gucci got into it with the ABCG Boys—" (AnyBody Can Get it) "over in East Atlanta, so he wanted extra protection for him and the Brick Squad." Wright finished referring to Gucci Mane's entourage and recording group. This was the information he pulled from his hip partner.

"That's understandable," Faqui said. "I've heard about them. After the fall of BMF, they were supposedly extorting Jeezy."

"Yeah, I know," Wright said, still not knowing or hip to rap aliases. If Faqui said his government name—Jerome Jenkins—he would've recognized him right away. But who the hell was Young Jeezy?

"Well let me show you the merchandise." With that, Faqui hit a hidden switch under his desk. When he did, a wall panel lifted to show a back-lit arsenal to the left of where Wright sat.

Faqui stood and approached the wall, followed by Wright. He had never seen such an extensive personal collection outside of the storage armory at work or a gun-expo.

There were the usual automatics; the AR-15s, Carbon 5s and of course the AK-47. But there were exotic and highly illegal River 22-250s, Mini 14s, 30-30s and Wright even peeped an M-4 Carbine. That was the police sniper rifle that took a .241 caliber round. Not to mention the hand guns; a Mac-9 and 10, a chrome Smith and Wesson .44 Anaconda and even more impressive, a .50 caliber gold Desert Eagle. Some of the weapons were tipped with illegal sound suppressors and silencers too.

"What is that?" Wright said as he pointed to a revolver with very large chambers. He had never seen anything like it. And he had been around guns his whole life. His father was a police officer.

"That's the revised Python. It's outlawed and technically, it doesn't exist except on paper. The Heckler and Koch design was too powerful to be approved. It's a handgun that shoots four twenty-gauge shotgun shells. When production stopped, Trinity Enterprises picked up the design and began making them for custom orders. Want to shoot it?" Faqui explained.

Wright didn't want to touch it let alone shoot it. It looked as if it would tear off someone's arm. He could see why it was illegal. But being illegal didn't mean it couldn't be found in the hands of a madman—or the streets of the inner-city ghettos.

"Tell Gucci he can set it off with this one." Faqui was holding an SKS with a collapsible stock.

"I got a confession," Wright admitted as he reached into his pocket.

"What? You need something bigger?" Faqui asked in all seriousness. He sounded as if he had a nuke hidden somewhere.

"*You're* going to have to see Gucci," Wright elaborated.

Sounding pleased as if this meant more money for him, Faqui replied, "Well bring him in anytime. I'll look all the way out."

"No, you're going to have to go to him."

"Where is he?" Faqui wanted to know.

Wright produced and showed his badge before he said, "In the DeKalb County jail on a probation violation."

# XIII
# SHADOW STALKING
# MONDAY, MARCH 7TH 2011
# SUNSET: 6:53 P.M.

THE MAN IN THE BLACK CAR COULD SMELL HIS VICTIMS. SOMETIMES HE DID SO even before he could see them. It was a far from pleasant odor, but uniquely distinct to his quarry. His quarry could also sniff its victims before they spotted them. But unlike the other man, this quarry smelled delicious.

The man dressed in black sat in the car and patiently stalked his oblivious quarry while his oblivious quarry stalked his victims.

The potential victims will never discern the complex dynamic of being a stalker—or the paradox of being stalked by a stalker who also was being stalked. Even if they did they would never understand. Mercifully, they never knew that they were being stalked in the first place. Had they known, their lives would have been changed forever. Just as their stalker's was on this dreadful night.

The Marta bus pulled up to one of its last stops of the night which was on the corner of Maple Street and Dee Drive.

The accordion door of the bus folded back to let the young couple exit into the cool night air. As they vacated the bus, little did they know eyes observed them.

Little did the watcher know he too was being even more closely scrutinized. The night was quiet except for the couple's footsteps on the pavement.

After the Marta bus had departed and its air brakes could not be heard relieving pressure anymore, the street was almost completely destitute of life. The abandoned street seemed ominous but did not in any way alarm the couple. Maple Street should have been more alive, it was only 10:36.

The light of the quarter-moon shined bright assisting the street lamps. A breeze gave the spring night a slight chill. Few stars accompanied the moon. The echo of the young couple's conversation could be heard reverberating off the houses they passed as they strolled the residential area of the urban neighborhood; College Park.

"Did you enjoy the movie Tiffany?" the man asked referring to the film they had just finished seeing at Lennox Mall. The motion picture was *New Moon*.

"I enjoyed being with you Jermaine," Tiffany replied to her best friend Courtny's on-again, off-again boyfriend. Yeah, she was a grimy one.

"I know that's right," he replied placing his arm around her shoulders as they walked the decrepit street to his duplex. "But for real, did you like it?" he wanted to know.

"I mighta liked it better if I had seen *Twilight* and the other one first," she answered. She was referring to *Eclipse*, the second movie based on the vampire book series. She wasn't into vampire flicks and had only gone to be with him.

"I doubt it. Either you were too scared to watch it because of the vampires, or you were too scared to enjoy it because you thought yo crazy-ass friend was gone catch you with me. Which one was it?" Jermaine asked laughing. He was aware that she feared Courtny.

Tiffany didn't think it was funny. "Boy stop," she said with a false smile.

Their stalker drew nearer to them. They didn't realize it from being engrossed in their conversation. Had they not been talking they still would have never exposed their stalker. Not until it was too late.

"So what would you do if she ever caught us in bed? Or found out we've been together behind her back for a while?" she countered, knowing Courtny would shoot them both.

The stalker drew closer.

"Shit, I'd get light. What you mean? I ain't ready to die," he said in a laughing tone but was dead serious.

"And just leave me like that?" Tiffany asked sassily.

*Hell yeah*, he thought. *You alright. But you ain't all that.* Not wanting to hurt her feelings or ruin his chances of physical gratification later, he replied, "Baby I was just playin'. I would never leave you."

With her arm wrapped around his waist she pulled him closer.

Their stalker drew close enough to spit on them.

They continued walking; their rhythmic footsteps masking the progress of their stalker. And their stalker's, stalker.

"So what would you do if a vampire crept up on us?" Jermaine asked in an ominously spooky tone.

"Boy stop. That was a fictional movie. And vampires don't exist."

Tell that to the one following you.

*Duh, it's a movie!* Jermaine thought, *See that's exactly why I would rather be with Courtny!* Aloud he said, "I mean hypothetically."

"I'd hit him with an old Popeyes two-piece and a biscuit," she said jabbing the air in front of her.

From behind them they both heard the deep voice as it challengingly said, "Yeah, well let's see!"

They both turned around startled by the sound of another person when they had been sure they were alone. Just as they did, a blinding light caused them to cover their eyes with their forearms. The light was accompanied by a singeing noise that sounded as if greasy hair was being burned by a hot comb, leaving the once fresh air permeated with that exact odor.

After a few moments both Jermaine and Tiffany lowered their arms, taking a couple seconds for their eyes to readjust to the darkness. What they saw was remarkable. Even more remarkable than the spontaneous light they had caught a glimpse of.

What they saw, was nothing.

No source of the blinding light. No source of the taunting voice.

"Did you just see that?" Tiffany asked Jermaine.

"Nope," he replied feigning ignorance. And ignorance was bliss.

"I'm for real," she encouraged. Jermaine was shaking his head. They started walking again. Then Tiffany blurted, "So I guess you didn't hear that shit either?" A challenging question.

"Hear what?" Jermaine replied not going to acknowledge any freaky shit.

Frustrated, Tiffany continued walking while murmuring, "Nothing."

After a few seconds Jermaine burst out laughing.

"What?" Tiffany smiled wanting to be in on the joke.

"Did it sound like Courtny finta get on yo ass?!" By now he was rolling. So was the man in black; hidden in the shadows.

# XIV
# RESTLESS NIGHTS

IT WAS WELL PAST TEN BY THE TIME WRIGHT MADE IT HOME. THIS CANCELLED HIS plan to call the hostage victims and find out if they had remembered something new; also his plan to compare and check for inconsistencies in their stories.

Wright had stayed at Connoisseur Import Autos until around nine. He had examined the scene as the officers bag-and-tagged the evidence, and listened as Faqui Muhammad ranted and raved about his rights and requested the presence of his attorney. He now resided on the 4th floor (felony arrests) of the DeKalb County jail. Not the 2nd (Child support and probation violations) where Radric Davis AKA Gucci Mane was collecting his three hots and a cot for a while.

After leaving CIA, Wright had cruised the cruel yet perversely comforting streets of Atlanta for over an hour.

He now sat in his warm leather recliner sipping three fingers of brandy as he reflected on the hectic day he had survived.

Ring. . . His phone rang bringing him back from his reflections. "Yeah?" he answered.

"The LT called to congratulate us on our successful bust of Faqui Muhammad." It was Thomas.

"Well, he won't be doing too much congratulating in a couple of days," Wright replied knowing the charges may be dropped.

"Yeah. Well I don't want to know how you did it then," she said more or less knowing how the tactics he employed were.

"Yeah, you're right," Wright conceded.

"Well I was just calling you to tell you good job," Thomas praised.

"Thanks," he said meaning it.

"You're welcome," she replied. They grew quiet for a moment before she broke the silence with, "Well, I'll see you tomorrow. Maybe we'll have as much luck on the Hijinks Heist case."

"Let's hope so," was his melancholy reply.

"Well. . . Bye," she sounded as if she wanted to say more.

"Bye," Wright said hanging up the phone. He wanted to say more too.

Wright refilled his brandy glass as he attempted to drown his sorrows; not let them drown him. He could have had a peaceful rest-filled night had she not called. But she did, and he didn't regret it. But he knew that as in this case like many other nights, his dreams would be haunted with wanton visions of her.

When he finally went to bed and rested his head on his pillow, he closed his eyes and drifted off.

Sometimes he hated when he was right. This was one of those times. Though the dreams were pleasant at night, when he awoke from them they caused his heart a pain that burned his soul.

Outside, the sparkling white 2010 Bentley Continental Supersport sat resting in his driveway next to his Ford; like an omen.

# DAY TWO

# I

# A PLEASANT SURPRISE
# TUESDAY, MARCH 8TH 2011
# SUNRISE: 5:33 A.M.

AFTER A LONG NIGH, THE SUN'S LIGHT PATTERN OF SHADED FOOTSTEPS TAP-danced across Shawnn Starr's face as he laid uncovered in his bed. This tender caress from the celestial center of our solar system caused him to rise from the waking dream he had been reliving. He had failed to set his alarm clock but the device signaled that it was 5:33 A.M.; so did the rising sun.

Mechanically Shawnn proceeded to his dojo and began his day as he did the others. He attempted to counter and balance the violent motions of the world.

Showered and shaved Shawnn arrived at Starr Private Investigators as fresh as he had the day before. It was another day in a long list of monotonous days that slipped through his grasp as time passed.

He wore khaki Dockers, a white Lacoste crew-shirt and very comfortable matching tan Oxfords. As he entered the office Shawnn was greeted by Jasmine who had on an elegant navy-blue womans' pants suit. She looked beautiful as usual as she handed him his morning papers.

As Shawnn went through his normal motions he was pleasantly surprised when he discovered a warming message on his yahoo account (*shawnnstarr@yahoo.com*). It correctly answered Shawnn's question; *Where will the light lead us?*

"Nowhere. Because it is we who shall lead the light."

Shawnn hit the reply icon on his screen and sent a message back to '*educatedAntoine@aol.com*' that read: *Give a time when the sun will rise?*

Beaming, Shawnn was thinking that the day looked a little less abysmal; less like the day before, and the day before, of the week before of the month before. This day would not be another day in the long list of monotonous days.

Little did he know how right he was in this assessment as he sat in the cool safe confines of his office. With the sun beaming in at him, Shawnn began reading his newspapers. He had some time to kill before his fateful meeting with his primary target.

# II

# OPPOSITES ATTRACT

SHAWNN STARR COULD FORGET TO SET HIS ALARM CLOCK AND LET THE SUN WAKE him. Worlds away Robbery/Homicide Detective Danny Wright could not afford this luxury. Unless of course he did not plan on being at work until around noon.

The alarm clock began its routine angry protest at 7:30 A.M. on the dot just as Wright had programmed it to do. Yet he still insisted on assaulting the faithful device as if it had offended him. It clattered to the floor.

Wright struggled for a toehold in his slow climb towards consciousness. Across Atlanta air conditioners dripped and rattled against the warm, angry spring. Just as in his restroom Wright dripped and rattled against protests of his unusually full bladder.

It took Wright seventeen minutes to shower, shave and dress so he found himself exiting and locking up his duplex at around 7:50. It was known to him that it took ten minutes to get to the DeKalb County Police Department, so he made it there at 8:00 sharp every day. But one caught red light or an accident somewhere along the way would completely throw off his schedule. Good thing his former police vehicle kept people cautious.

Turning to face the bright red glowing orb in the sky as it peeked over the horizon, Wright thought the sun looked angry. It had a right to be angry, due to the underappreciated fact that it was the giver of all life on the planet Earth. Without it, where would we be? Simple, eternal darkness; eternal cold darkness.

Wright passed the luxury coupe on his way to his not-so-luxury sedan. Momentarily he thought about driving the Bentley, but how would that look? A homicide detective with a quarter-million dollar car would be as suspicious as an Arab on a plane to New York. *Sir, can we check your turban?*

Wright did not want to be labeled as the bad-cop who accepted bribes—he already was labeled as a bad-cop, he just didn't want to add the accepting bribes part to his title. He didn't want to flash unexplained wealth. *Where'd you get that, don't you make like seventy grand a year?* Sixty if he's lucky. More times than less he's not lucky.

The Ford started with aggression as if to announce to the adjacent car that he was there. Due to Faqui's steady personification of the Bentley—*she* this, *let her* that—Wright now viewed his Ford as an ugly male who had led a hard life. Even though its name was feminine—Victoria. He—the bland Ford, and she—the beautiful Bentley, made an unlikely but formidable pair. Who would own both cars?

Just as he—the bland Detective Wright, and she—his beautiful partner Thomas, made an unlikely but just as formidable pair. As they say and has been proven with magnets;opposites attract. Wright headed to work with these thoughts in mind.

# III
# STEAK 'N SHAKE DOWN

SHAWNN ARRIVED AT THE SAME STEAK 'N SHAKE RESTAURANT AT AROUND THE same time as he arrived the previous day. It seemed crowded with around the same customers as the day before. The waitress who served him saw him as he entered and graced him with a wave along with a pretty smile. Shawnn nodded acknowledgement to her but instead of heading over to dine in her section, he chose to sit at the bar.

Shawnn was seated a couple stools down from where Hamilton had sat about 24 hours ago. In lieu of a large meal he settled on a vanilla milkshake which he immediately paid for. He didn't know if the woman would return, but he wanted to be prepared to pursue her if she did. He hoped she did. But he believed in neither hope, chance, nor coincidence.

The milkshake arrived. It was in a tall frosty glass topped with warm fudge and a large maraschino cherry. Shawnn dug in, enjoying how the cool desert soothed his parched throat.

His target walked in when he was a quarter from completing his drink that was so thick Shawnn needed to use a spoon on the first half. Harold Hamilton was just as obese as he was the previous day only now he was wearing atrocious corduroy pants. They were held up by suspenders. *Whatever he lacks in fashion sense, he more than makes up for in pounds,* Shawnn thought as the squat man managed to wedge himself between the bar and stool. He burdened the stool three seats down from where

Shawnn sat. Shawnn hadn't brought his hidden camera today because what he planned didn't entail taking pictures.

⟨⟩⟨⟩

Having already devoured a plate of spaghetti and a plate of French fries—both being smothered in rich thick ranch dressing—Hamilton's nachos arrived. Along with their arrival came the gorgeous brunette woman with the beautiful skin tone. She glowed like the full moon on a cloudless night.

Today she dressed conservative with very nice formfitting blue jeans and a powder-pink shirt. The shirt was cut provocatively low in the front and had fashionable ruffles lacing the collar and sleeves. It looked classy but also expensive. She wore pointed-toe heels that matched the shirt like they were cut from the same cloth. Resting between her exposed cleavage was a thin gold-rope necklace with a tiny matching cross for a charm.

Shawnn experienced a want in his heart that he never felt for any woman—period. He wasn't cold, just too focused on his goals to fall in love. Especially with a woman he didn't know—or never spoke one word to.

She sat two stools away from Shawnn between him and Hamilton. Her faint perfume drifted into Shawnn's area tantalizing his sense of smell with promises of pleasure. His longing grew deeper as his nostrils flared.

Today Shawnn heard their conversation as he digested his milkshake. Their discussion was harder to digest.

"Do you have what I want?" she asked skipping the pleasantries and getting to business.

"Not exactly," Hamilton replied wiping crumbs from his beard.

"So you set up this meeting with me last night under false pretenses?" she asked with frustration in her voice.

"I wouldn't say that," was Hamilton's cryptic reply.

"You're wasting my time," the beautiful woman stated as she got up to leave.

Hamilton, remembering the look in her eyes the day before, didn't try to restrain her. He stopped her departure with, "I couldn't find the information you want, but I did find you someone who can."

She reseated herself with a look on her face that said *elaborate.*

Shawnn listened to this exchange. For some strange reason he was relieved and pleased to find out that the woman was not romantically involved with the style-less blob seated next to her. Their involvement sounded businesslike. Shawnn was curious to find out what that business was.

"Who?" she inquired when Hamilton didn't continue.

"The CEO of Trinity Enterprises, Cedric Montgomery," Harold Hamilton stated proudly. "I was able to schedule you a brief meeting with him," he said as if the rendezvous was arranged using the limitless clout he possessed.

"When and where," she urged.

For a moment Hamilton's conscience warned him of the danger and the bad vibes he received about setting up a meeting with Montgomery. It appeared as if doom loomed on the horizon. Then the other side of him—his adversarial conscience—reminded him of the five hundred dollars he was already spending in his mind, doomed to be splurged.

"Tomorrow," he began. "At his office on the 30th floor of Trinity Enterprises at 2:30. Do you know where that is?" he finished, sealing the doom to come. "And the money?"

"Yes," she replied as she gathered her pocketbook and stood up from the stool to make her exit.

Dropping chili sauce on his shirt from the nachos in route to his mouth, Hamilton asked, "Where are you going?"

"That my indulgent rat, is none of your concern. We have nothing else to discuss," she responded.

"What about the rest of my money," Hamilton protested.

"I believe the deal was the half you already received, and the other half when I received certain information. Since I have not received that information I owe you nothing," was her terse explanation.

As she turned to leave she made brief eye contact with Shawnn who was about to leave also. She was gorgeous. Her eyes were a honey-green shade that today was closer to honey than it was to green as it had been yesterday. She was beautiful. But beauty was in the eyes of the beholder. Or in her case beauty was the holder of the eyes.

Shawnn was once again struck by the uncanny sense that he knew the woman as he mentally reviewed his notes. *Cedric Montgomery; Trinity Enterprises; CEO 30th floor; 2:30 tomorrow; information?*

She left. So did Shawnn, leaving Hamilton to continue raising his blood pressure and clogging his arteries. One of the thirty six percent of the growing category of obese Americans.

After what seemed a proper lapse in time to get to her vehicle Shawnn realized she either wasn't leaving yet, or she parked somewhere else. Barely in time he saw her turn onto Parker Boulevard at a quick walking pace.

*So that was how she disappeared the last time; she was walking,* Shawnn thought. He attempted to close the growing gap between them.

He did. Then he was in pursuit mode.

Though his client had worried about her husband's infidelity, Shawnn still followed the women just in case. Not only to cover his bases, but because he was curious to know more about her. The slight sense of déjà vu he felt around her increased his intrigue about the woman who proved to be very elusive.

Shawnn was having a hard time keeping pace with the woman while attempting to stay back at a safe distance. He wondered how she even maintained the brisk walk in the heels she wore. He thanked himself for wearing his suede Oxfords because he wasn't sure any of his Faragamos or Stacey Adams could have withstood this torture.

Shawnn continued following the woman for several blocks before he realized that she wasn't traveling to a stationary destination. She was traveling in a series of complex circles. This afforded him a chance to grow intimate with and appreciate his city.

In 1837, a town called Terminus was founded at the southeastern end of the Western and Atlantic Railroad. The town soon developed into a busy trade and transportation center. In 1845, J. Edgar Thompson, a railroad engineer, renamed the town Atlanta after the Western and Atlantic railroad that made him prosperous.

During the civil war (1861-1865), Atlanta served as a Confederate supply depot. Union troops led by General William T. Sherman captured the city and burned most of its buildings. Since then, Atlanta, Georgia has had several periods—especially in the 1960's—of industrial expansion and constructional growth. All of this was clear as Shawnn admired his view of the city. And the view of the woman he pursued.

Swayed by the woo of her hips or wooed by the sway of her curves, Shawnn grew confused. As they approached the corner of Vine and Davis Street for at least the third time, the woman stopped and turned around doing a 180 towards Shawnn. She had glanced behind herself occasionally throughout their track but nothing thus far had been this blatant.

Most other pedestrians had returned to their jobs but some still lingered. Notwithstanding, the woman now had an unrestricted view of Shawnn. He thought so far she'd been oblivious to his presence. Apparently not. Or maybe she just felt the tingle down her spine announcing the holes he was staring into her back. . .side.

Shawnn quickly kneeled down and began fumbling with his shoe-strings as if tying them. He hoped he seemed natural. After the Oxford was retied Shawnn felt ample time had passed for her to have resumed her pointless course. He chanced a glance up.

Surprise. She was staring at him with no innuendo or candor. Her eyes pierced him all the way to his inner being; to his very soul.

Does she know she has a tail? Does she know that he'd been trailing behind her for the past hour or so trying to stay invisible at a thirty to fifty yard interval?

His mistake would have been in turning away from her stare. But that is how most are trained in covert surveillance. This is so they keep their face from becoming too familiar to their target.

But he was not most. He was insidious in every sense of the word; sly, beguiling, cunning and treacherous. All of which concealed his underlying tone of intelligence.

After diverting his eyes from her and back to his shoe to inspect his handy work, Shawnn was surprised to find that when he stood up she was gone. Shawnn hop-trotted to the corner of the block she had to have turned down. He did this as quickly as he could without drawing any undue attention to himself. Just as he got to the corner he peered around the building, getting there in the nick of time to glimpse her turning from the sidewalk onto the next block of Terrace Boulevard.

*Damn she's fast*, Shawnn thought as he weaved through the few pedestrians straggling on Davis Road. He arrived at that corner almost at a full sprint he nearly didn't see her head ducking into the kiosk of the Northbound Wheeler Avenue Station. Shawnn jogged across the street dodging cars as he did, and took the steps two at a time descending into the subway.

Shawnn hopped the turnstile and proceeded to the loading platform. People milled about as they waited for the northbound train. Shawnn searched faces inconspicuously but with thorough care. He did not see the woman anywhere. He lost her. Or to be exact, she lost him.

Across the track the southbound train was leaving the platform. Shawnn continued searching. He heard the squeal of protest from the railcar as it started motion, gaining speed on its way to its next destination.

Hearing the train come to life Shawnn glanced up at it. The train cars passed one after the other with no distinction—until he saw her. She was seated on the southbound train glancing out the window over her shoulder at him.

How did she get on that train? From this side especially? She would have had to go back up the stairs and crossed Wheeler Avenue again, surely passing him in the attempt. Or to cross the thirty foot expanse between the platforms on a parallel axis she would have had to navigate over the two 750 volt rails. The slightest touch from either one will instantly kill a man. Then she would have had to climb the five feet back onto the other platform on the other side.

She didn't have the time to do either. Furthermore, she'd have been spotted by him in the course of either action. Plus the southbound train had boarded when he descended into the station. The woman only had a ten or fifteen second head-start on him.

In addition to these dilemmas Shawnn now wondered if she had planned this. Had she spotted him earlier and known she was being followed the whole time? Did this in turn cause her to wander aimlessly waiting until right when she knew that the train would be departing? Then lead him down the opposite kiosk and seemingly board the train from the other platform? Is she that clever? Could she be that methodical?

*Nah*, Shawnn thought. It had to be a coincidence. Even though he did not believe that in the complicated structure of the universe there was anything left to chance.

Newton's famous law: for every action there is an equal but opposite reaction.

She planned this. . . deception.

His suspicions were confirmed when their eyes met across the expanse and between the people waiting on the northbound subway car. She was looking at him with a bemused expression on her face. She waved from the window with a look that said *Better luck next time!* But based upon her actions, Shawnn knew with decisive certainty that there would never be another next time. At least not in this life.

# IV
# NO PAIN NO GAIN

On Atlanta's southside in the urban neighborhood of Decatur, sat Tyson's Gym. It was situated between a liquor store and a Roscoe's Chicken and Waffles. The gym was named after the former heavyweight Champion of the World. He had funded the building for the recreation of inner city youths and to keep them off of the streets. This was before he dined on ears.

Inside the gym on the outer perimeter, a pair of boxers trained using the speed and heavy punching bags. Near the large center ring a teenager jumped rope. Sweat dripped off of his shirtless body as he enjoyed an entertaining show. Inside the four cornered ring two people put on the engrossing show. They were wearing kickboxing gloves and protective headgear.

"Gotcha," Thomas said to Wright. They always worked out once or twice a week in one form or another whether it be jogging, weightlifting or as in the case of today, boxing. They did this to stay in shape.

Wright got up from the padded mat and put up his guard. No sooner did he do so did a vicious right come towards his face. It was followed by a kick in the ribs from Thomas as she snarled, "Come on!"

Wright dodged the punch but the kick to the ribs knocked the wind from him. He grabbed the offending leg with his right arm and keeping it pressed against his side, Wright returned a punch with his left hand which was ducked under easily.

"Don't hold back!" Thomas said spinning out of his grasp. He wasn't. Though she told him this every time they sparred he had stopped doing that months ago. She didn't believe him. She thought he was being soft on her.

Thomas was a hard woman. Though she had a soft side, when it came to physical strength she was tough. And whatever she lacked in strength she made up for in speed and dexterity.

Jab, jab, uppercut. Shawnn back peddled. Then he went in and connected with a quick three-piece combination that didn't seem to faze Thomas as much as he thought it should have.

She returned to combat with a knee to his thigh and then she swept his feet out from under him. Once again he was on his back.

Wright had wanted to spar because the physical conditioning was a good way to have stress worked out of him. He got to his feet again and the match continued. The man who had been jumping rope now stood watching them with interest—more like amusement. They chose this particular gym for its seclusion and privacy. Just as when they lifted weights they went to a private gym instead of the free one that was open to detectives and officers.

Thomas didn't like the way the other man ogled her physique. She also didn't care for too many spectators. This was good for Wright too because he didn't want his colleagues seeing him get his ass kicked. Just as it was being done now.

For a few moments they were going toe-to-toe boxing. But Thomas, being 5'6, 113 pounds, didn't have near the reach or strength of Wright who was about six feet and weighed 195 pounds. So she had to fight her fight. Her footwork was nice and she could slam a man three times her size if the need arose.

High kick, high kick, sweep. This time Wright jumped over the sweep and closed the gap, all but making her vicious yet beautiful legs useless.

She tried to knee him but he deflected it. The rage on her face was clear. She hated to lose—but looked so sexy doing it.

She had on loose-fitting gray sweatpants and a black sports bra; other than her gloved hands, that was it. Her exposed toes were long and beautiful. Her revealed midriff looked exactly how it did in his dreams. The small inny bellybutton was framed by a flat but well-toned stomach. Her breast filled the sports bra nicely, and the sweat that ran down the front of it caused her whole body to glisten.

*Damn she was beau*—just then she tried to elbow him with her right forearm. Wright caught it as he was trained then turned her around, putting her in a belly-to-back bear-hug—that wasn't training.

Wright had wanted to fight off his stress and lust, however it didn't seem to be helping. Actually it was the exact opposite. The smell of her hair mingling with her natural scent and the musky smell of sweat, plus the intimate contact of her buttocks against his groin was torture. He grew aroused. That was why he was being bested. He couldn't focus under this pressure—no man could. At least not focus on self-defense; maybe self-indulgence.

Some way they always wound up like this. Her butt pressed against his growing manhood. It never failed. He wondered sometimes if she did this on purpose; grappling. It was her best defense against his heavy blows and gave her a slight advantage over his power. In this position though it didn't appear that way, she was in control. He knew this because they always wound up this way.

Wright didn't know if she had just been besting him the whole time or if he allowed her to get him in this position because of the over-her-shoulder view of her rack it provided. Or the intimately nice feel of her derrière against his member. Either way, whenever they sparred at least three times they would be in this same position, with him bear-hugging her from behind. But he knew she had the advantage from experience.

He wondered if she could feel him growing aroused.

Just as always around this time she began her maneuver. Wright knew it was coming but was powerless to stop it. That, or he let it happen just so he could be close to her—and so she'd continue to do it.

The advantage she had was him being an inch shy of six feet so he had a higher center of gravity than her. She was a half-foot shorter with more stability. So inevitably, the arm he had grasped to spin her away from him was over-her-shoulder. Without exerting much energy or using a lot of force, she ducked down and pulled forward.

One second Wright was viewing the mat and big breasts from above; the next he was viewing the ceiling and big breasts from below.

She finished this highly effective maneuver with the same phrase she always muttered as she kneeled above his head in victory.

"Gotcha!" Thomas was proud of her achievement. Resting on his back, so was Wright.

The man who had been jumping rope was now holding his side in gut-wrenching laughter. Inwardly, so was Wright.

# V
# BETTER LUCK NEXT TIME

*BETTER LUCK NEXT TIME*, ECHOED SHAWNN'S THOUGHTS AS THE TRAIN ACCELERATED into the darkened subway tunnel. But he knew deep down in his heart that there would never be a 'next time.' So he had to make this one count.

The northbound train could now be heard as it was coming close to exiting the tunnel that the southbound train with the woman was entering. Waiting passengers grew anxious with its impending arrival while Shawnn grew desperate. The view of the woman waving from the window at him as the train departed was engraved in his mind like the inscription of a tombstone. Shawnn wouldn't let it be his last vision of her.

Shawnn knew he didn't have time to climb into the ditch and latch on to the departing train before the northbound train turned him into ground beef. Furthermore, even if he could, the southbound train with the woman on it was moving too fast. It accelerated to the seventy miles per hour that the northbound train was traveling at in the opposite direction towards the platform. There were three carts left visible on southbound train the woman was on.

What should he do? He knew about the back loading panel of the last cart of every train, but how could he get there? If he attempted to jump from the platform to the train—which was over thirty feet—and miscalculated, he'd hit the side of it and be killed. Or if the impact didn't kill him the arrival of the northbound train would.

If he jumped too late he would miss the panel, landing on the dreaded third rail. That would send 750 volts of unrestricted, unresisted current through his body; another instant way to die.

The lights of the northbound train could now be seen reflecting off of the other train and the walls and ceiling of the tunnel.

Shawnn had to decide and he had to do it quick. Otherwise, the elusive woman—he still didn't even know her name—would be lost to him forever. With two carts left to go on the train and seconds before the other train arrived, Shawnn made a decision. And he knew with a life or death certainty, he had to time it right.

He glanced around the platform and saw that nobody was paying him any attention because they were so intent on the arriving train and their future destinations.

There went the last train of the southbound as the northbound car now came into full view with the sound of. . . a subway train. The electricity that flowed through the third rail could be heard as it perfumed the air with static.

It was now or never. With a final glance around and a silent prayer, Shawnn dashed down the concrete terminal to the edge of the platform with desperation and leapt.

He leapt over 750 volts of killing power and glided through the air only inches away from over forty-five tons of cold hard steel traveling at a speed in excess of seventy miles per hour.

Thirty feet from where he left the platform Shawnn landed with a dull thud on the last dock of the final car of the departing southbound train. He felt the wind of the northbound cart as it pulled into the terminal.

He finally let out the breath he had been holding.

Shawnn glanced into the back window of the shaky cart. Apparently nobody had seen his brush with death, or the near fatal leap. He deduced his target was more than five cars up, so he parted the rear emergency doors and entered the cart.

Shawnn was met with a few curious stares, but for the most part nobody paid him any mind. He casually took a seat next to a beautiful young woman who was engrossed in a conversation on her phone. He pulled his Apple iPhone from his pants pocket. After scrolling through his electronic phone book he hit the send button on the name he had sought.

"Starr Private Investigators," Jasmine answered in her gaily exuberant voice. Shawnn informed her that he didn't know when he'd be back so she had better order out. She thanked him and told him that Mrs. Hamilton had called inquiring after any new developments.

*Yeah, my newly developed fear of subways* he thought but replied he'd call Mrs. Hamilton when he returned to the office. He hung up and waited on the next stop to see if the woman would be departing.

A few moments later they were at the next station. Shawnn observed the passengers exiting the train, hoping to spot the woman.

Oblivious to his surroundings, he viewed many strange, exotic and. . . ugly faces. But he did not see the woman he was intent on following.

The train resumed its rocky motion. Shawnn settled back into his seat making eye contact with the bright skinned, beautiful woman in the seat next to him. Pretty, but young. There was nothing to be gained mentally, psychologically, emotionally or financially from her. But she sure looked to be able to elevate him and build physically—on many levels.

She smiled at Shawnn; he returned the smile with eighteen percent interest. He was intent on his mission. He maintained a mental image of his target in his mind's eye as he pondered where he had seen her.

At the next stop Shawnn gazed out of the window of the train, only to be disappointed again. The young woman in the seat next to him stood up placing a folded piece of paper into his hand before departing the train. She was engrossed in her cell phone conversation.

Shawnn unfolded the small slip of paper to reveal a phone number and a name scribbled on it in a cutesy script. The name read; *Courtny*, with a small heart for an '*o*'. He peered out of the window of the now departing train and saw the woman waving her empty hand—the other was still being occupied with her cell phone. When he met her eyes she winked and mouthed 'call me.'

At the train's next destination, Shawnn was rewarded for tempting fate by finally catching the woman leaving the cart. She seemed unaware that he had been able to board the train behind her as she stepped onto the platform. He knew that she could spot a tail and prove to be very elusive so he stayed well back from her to avoid detection.

They were at the Peachtree Street Station. Shawnn noticed as she exited in a not so brisk walk. The afternoon sun was bright. Shawnn enjoyed it as he followed the woman at a safe distance. Moments later she entered a public parking garage. Shawnn posted up across the street with some teenagers who had cut school. They were engrossed in a dice game; he was engrossed in anticipation.

The minutes passed by as he observed every vehicle that left the garage. When he spotted her, she was in a new model navy-blue Chevy Impala. As she turned left onto Peachtree Street Shawnn mentally noted the license plate number with Cobb County tags.

Shawnn thought that it must be his lucky day as he joined the teenagers' dice game. He laid a twenty-dollar bill he had taken from his wallet on the ground then announced, "Let me get a fade."

"Here old school," said one of the youngsters as they passed him the dice.

*If only he knew*, Shawnn thought as he rattled and shook them in his hand a few seconds before releasing them toward the side of the building. The dice bounced against the brick wall before tumbling into a rapid spin. When the dice came to a rest, one showed five dots on its face, the other two.

"Seven," Shawnn proclaimed victoriously as he gathered a few crumpled bills off of the ground. Yes, it must be his lucky day. "Bet back?" he asked.

# VI
# NO FACE NO CASE

AFTER SHOWERING AWAY THE EFFECTS OF PHYSICAL EXERTION, DETECTIVES WRIGHT and Thomas were now in his Crown Vic on the way back to the police department—presumably to do actual police work. It had been thirty hours since the Highjinks Heist and they were no closer to solving the case. They knew that this case, as in most crimes had the highest possibility—eighty-five percent—of being solved in the first forty-eight hours. After that only fifteen percent of crimes were solved, so they had to get to work. They couldn't afford not to solve this.

The two detectives were discussing the previous day's interviews of the victims when they heard the dispatcher request an ambulance and a squad car to Forest Park. There had been a man who attempted suicide by jumping from the window of his eighth floor apartment. Wright and Thomas were in the area so they felt obligated to investigate the crime.

Suicide was one of the few crimes where the perpetrator was both the victim and the victimizer. All suicides had to be investigated for any hint of foul play. Holidays had the highest suicide rate. People killed themselves in the hundreds of thousands every day for any assorted number of reasons. The loss of a job to the loss of a spouse; from the inheritance of debt to the inheritance of a life threatening illness. Many people didn't want to go through extended pain or suffering. Some folks wanted to feel like they controlled their own destinies. Whatever the reason, suicide separated human beings from animals. Animals had an inbred instinct, an unshakeable want to live no matter how bleak the situation. Humans had no respect for life; not even their own.

When Wright arrived at the fifteen story apartment complex in Forest Park called Tower Villas, he and Thomas noticed the leaving ambulance. It had no emergency beacons blaring so they were confused. The emergency dispatcher had said that the suicide was attempted from the eighth story. So even if he had lived he'd be in critical condition, causing the ambulance to rush the man to the hospital. So why were they leaving so fast? Even if the man succeeded the ambulance would've had to wait for the medical examiner to release the body.

Wright and Thomas headed to the front of the building. They passed a parked black-and-white on the curb. As they were about to enter the complex they saw the occupants of the squad car exiting the apartments.

One was Officer Brewer, the cop from the bank heist who'd let the criminals get away. Wright didn't know the other one but he could recognize the disgruntled looks on their faces.

"Hey Wright," Brewer acknowledged him and Thomas with a nod. "You detectives would be wasting your time if—" just then Brewer's phone rang, interrupting whatever he was about to say. "Excuse me," he said taking a few steps to the side. Wright still overheard his half of the conversation.

"Yeah, what is it?" he asked the person on the other end. "What's the number?" He took a pen from his pocket and wrote on his hand. "When I get to my car I'll do it. Just give me a minute," he hung up and returned to where Wright, Thomas and the other officer still stood. The other officer hadn't spoken a word.

"Sorry about that," Brewer apologized. "As I was saying, you guys are wasting your time."

Thomas would have normally corrected his use of 'guys' to describe them but she held her tongue. . . a first for her.

"Why is that?" Wright inquired.

"We got the same call that y'all heard, but it's bogus," Brewer said.

"What do you mean?" Wright didn't like how Brewer was beating around the bush.

"Long story short," he began. "It's a crazy old lady inventing stories. Take my word for it." Brewer had dismissed the claim.

"So nobody jumped from a window?" Thomas spoke for the first time.

"If he did we sure didn't find a body." Wright looked at him. Feeling analyzed and not liking it Brewer invited, "She is the landlord and stays in 1-A. Don't believe me check it out for yourself." With that said he proceeded to their squad car, motioning his partner to follow.

No, Wright didn't believe him; and he did intend to see for himself.

Wright rapped on the door marked '1-A' by a gold faceplate. The plaque right below it read 'Superintendent.' It took a few seconds for an older woman in her late 70's to answer the door in a bathrobe and house slippers. She was white with a close cropped afro of silver curls on her head. Her frail body showed the wear and tear of a long life.

"It's about time. Come in, come in." She opened the door wide enough to allow them entry. The room was small. It may have been larger had it not been filled with the accumulated trinkets of longevity. Ceramic figures sat on every available space, and on top of a floor model TV was a 13-inch TV. The couch and two chairs were covered with plastic but in no way matched each other or the non-existent color scheme of the living room. A cat hopped over Wright's feet on its way to the kitchen; which had enough room to open the oven or the refrigerator—not both at one time.

Wright absorbed this in his investigator's eye but came to no conclusion of the old lady's mental state. She began speaking.

"Well I'm glad real investigators came. Those other two assholes couldn't figure out where their dicks were if they were pissing."

Vulgar—one sign of old age.

"So what happened Ms. . ." Thomas was asking.

"Misses. Mrs. Jennine Spears. My husband has been dead five years though his memory still lives on. I talk to his ghost sometimes. We always watch *Wheel of Fortune*."

Delusional—sign number two of old age.

"What about the man who jumped out the window?" Wright pressed.

"Oh yeah, he just flew like—I forgot to offer y'all something to drink. I know investigating is hard work because—" she started to ramble again but Thomas cut her off.

"No thank you," she spoke for both of them. Then, "So he was trying to kill himself?"

"Yep. Jumped right out the window like he could fly," she replied.

The cat trounced back into the room as if he owned the place. If the cat hair on almost all the surfaces held any weight, he did.

"Where was this," Wright said encouraging the old woman.

"Upstairs, I'll take you to—I forgot to offer y'all something to drink. I know y'all get tired."

Forgetfulness—sign number three.

"Please show us the window," Thomas interrupted.

After grabbing a set of keys Mrs. Spears led them up the stairs. She hadn't bothered to put on something less revealing or gruesome than the bathrobe before leaving her tiny apartment. Not minding to expose or disgust others with your indecency—sign number four.

The apartments didn't have a working elevator so they had to ascend the steps with Mrs. Spears slowly; one step at a time. While Wright wondered if she would make the trip at all, somewhere between flights four and seven Thomas was able to coax the story from the woman.

"It had been a while since I seen Jeremy, so—" Mrs. Spears was explaining before she was interrupted.

"Who's that? Your dead husband," Thomas asked in seriously.

"No silly, it's the tenant," she responded as if to a child.

"What's his full name?" Wright asked.

"Jeremy Taylor." Wright wrote the name as she continued. "Last month he hadn't come in to pay his rent. See I collect rent from the first to the seventh of each month, after that it's late. Jeremy was a young free-lance photographer, so sometimes he couldn't always come up with the rent on time. He was twenty-one. I knew this because he'd sometimes sit and watch *Jeopardy* with me and Matthew."

"So Matthew is the dead husband you watch TV with?" Wright asked.

"Y'all don't pay attention. My husband and I watch *Wheel of Fortune*. Matthew is my cat. But Jeremy was a sweet boy. When he didn't pay his rent on the seventh I assumed he'd bring it when he got it. I hadn't seen him in a while, so I called and stopped by to check on him. He was never home. I figured he was away on a trip or photo assignment but he never went so long without checking on me. And he would have told me if he was leaving. Yesterday was the seventh. When he didn't bring me his rent this time, I decided to find out why."

By now they had made it to the eighth floor. Though Mrs. Spears didn't seem winded she did appear paler. Wright wondered if it was the climb or the telling of the events that had her shook.

They walked down the clean but deteriorating corridor to come to a stop in front of a door marked '8-D.' Mrs. Spears took the keys and opened the door allowing them to enter behind her. She began retelling the events again.

"Jeremy was always such a neat boy, so this surprised me."

The room was in complete disarray. It looked as if a wild animal had been turned loose and forced to be confined to the tiny apartment. Before, Wright had thought the landlady's living quarters looked small because of the junk she possessed, but looking at Jeremy's cell—that's what it appeared to be—he realized they must all be that way. Wright felt a sense of claustrophobia coming. Even in Atlanta with their pursuit to expand rapidly with hastily built high-rise apartments, this was small. Whoever built this place tried to squeeze every penny out of every square foot.

The couch was overturned. Clothes were piled in heaps everywhere. Dishes clogged the sink with clutter. A pigsty could have been the Hyatt Regency compared to the filth of this apartment. Mrs. Spears was telling what happened again.

"When I came I knocked, but no one answered. I thought I heard something from behind the door but I wasn't sure."

There was a draft blowing through the small space. It ruffled Mrs. Spears robe revealing some of an orangutan-titty. Either she didn't notice or didn't care, because she continued as if the blue varicose veins across her dried-up breasts weren't exposed.

"When I saw this I became worried. I almost jumped out of my skin when I heard a noise coming from the bedroom."

It was the smallest room Wright had ever seen. The bed was a full-sized mattress but filled the room like a double king. Wright now saw where the draft came from. The single window that was about three feet squared was wide open.

Standing in the doorway still explaining, Mrs. Spears continued in an eerie voice. "When I opened the bedroom door I saw Jeremy kneeling in the window. It was as if he was waiting on me. When he turned and saw me he said, 'I'll tell your husband you said hi', then he jumped." A silent tear graced her cheek as if she was reliving the pain and fear she felt at seeing the young man jump to his doom.

Wright went to the window inspecting the area as Thomas continued to question Mrs. Spears. "Did he have any reason to take his life?" said Thomas in a sympathetic voice.

"No. He was a sweet boy who'd been on his own after graduating. Any troubles he had could have been easily solved," Mrs. Spears answered.

"Did he have a girlfriend or any frequent visitors?"

"If so he never told or showed me," she sadly answered.

"So you were sweating him about the rent?" Thomas asked curiously.

"No, it wasn't like that. I would have given him more time." Another tear.

"How much did he owe you?"

"About twelve-fifty," Mrs. Spears replied.

"Twelve hundred dollars. I've seen people murdered for less," Thomas stated.

"What are you suggesting?" Mrs. Spears spat with more tears.

"I'm just saying that it's a good motive for murder. It's not like I am assuming you got him to look out the window then pushed him," Thomas implied.

As Wright had been listening to this he examined the area outside the window. He noticed other windows had air conditioning units that dripped condensation to the concrete sidewalk far below. He noticed flower pots in some windows but at the bottom of the hundred foot drop, there were no splattered remains of a suicide victim. There was nothing to show that a man had plunged to his death from eight stories. Wright interrupted Thomas' interrogation.

"What happened after he jumped?" Wright asked. Thomas took her cue and went to investigate the window for herself.

Mrs. Spears straightened her face before replying, "I went to a neighbor's house and called 9-1-1."

"So you didn't see him hit the pavement?" Wright inquired.

"I didn't want to," she said in seriousness.

"So for all you know he could have just pretended to jump, then hung on the ledge of the window until he was sure you had left?"

"No. He wouldn't do that. And if he did I'd have seen him because I never left the floor until the officers came. There's one way in and one way out of these apartments."

Fire hazard.

"When the officers came what happened?" Wright wondered aloud.

"They pretty much looked out the window and dismissed me as crazy when they said they didn't see a body."

*Yep, what we're about to do.*

"I'm old, not stupid," Mrs. Spears said matter-of-factly.

Senility—sign number five of old age.

"Why do you think there was no body?"

"You're the detective, you tell me." She replied. Sarcasm—sign number six.

"Are you sure you saw Jeremy..." Wright pulled out his notepad, "Taylor?"

"As sure as you are you have a dick," she answered, not sure that he did.

Thomas shut the window and returned to Wright's side. As much as he didn't want to agree with Brewer, he had to admit that this was a waste of time—and that the lady was crazy too; watching *Wheel of Fortune* with her cat and dead husband's ghost.

"What was Jeremy wearing?" Wright wondered.

With a slight pause to bring back the memory she said, "A white T-shirt and blue jeans."

"Shoes?" Thomas intoned for Wright.

"I wasn't looking at his footwear as he leapt to his fucking doom!"

Wright went back to the window raising it as he asked, "So he was already standing here waiting when you came in?"

"Good to know you were paying attention." More sarcasm.

"No suicide note," Thomas asked.

"If it is then it's buried beneath this mess. What are you gonna do?"

"Well there's nothing we can do. There's no body to speak of and we can't file a missing persons report until after twenty-four hours. You said you saw him today." Thomas glanced at her watch, "So we'll be in contact with you at around 2:30 tomorrow.

Wright didn't find the shoe prints on the ledge he was looking for but he did find something even more interesting in the wooden frame.

"So what do I do with his things?" Mrs. Spears asked worriedly.

"Evict him. You said he hasn't paid his rent in two months so you can legally take his property and sell it for debts owed. All you need to do is fill out the 18-52 form at the courthouse." Thomas suggested.

Wright thought that the woman was old and senile at first until she said, "Well, I will do that after me and Fica watch *Who Wants to be a Millionaire.*"

"So Fica is the name of your dead husband," Thomas asked confused.

"No, his name is Phil. Fica is my plant silly," Mrs. Spears replied in honesty.

Wright had accepted the fact that she talked to her dead husband to ease the pain but the seventh and final sign of not just old age, but of being crazy is; talking to plants. Wright shook his head in wonder, contemplating if to take this crazy old lady seriously. No face, no case.

# VII
# NO REPLY

SHAWNN STARR RETURNED TO SPI AT AROUND 3:00 AFTER BEATING THE TEENAGERS out of six hundred forty dollars. He had called an acquaintance—Officer Brewer—about running the woman's plates for an address for him. Shawnn was still awaiting a return call. Jasmine had ordered a pizza, so Shawnn dinned on four slices of meat-lovers as he checked his emails. There still had been no reply.

Not long after the pizza was gone Jasmine buzzed in. "Mrs. Hamilton is on line two," she said.

"Put her through. . . Hello Mrs. Hamilton. How are you?" Shawnn answered.

"Have you made any progress?" Mrs. Hamilton asked, skipping formalities with venom.

"I do have good news for you," was Shawnn in his Bryant Gumbel tone.

"That's good to hear. What might it be?" Mrs. Hamilton sounded as if grains of sand were permanently lodged in the folds of her vagina.

"I was able to follow the woman I observed with your husband at lunch yesterday. Rest assured, he's not cheating on you. They have some sort of business transaction going on," Shawnn explained.

"Where does she live?" Mrs. Hamilton asked; anticipation laced her voice.

"I didn't follow her home, I followed her to the car," Shawnn replied wincing as soon as the words left his mouth. "But I will have her address soon. I'm waiting on the call. I think you misunderstood. Your husband is not having an affair with this woman. They are bartering over some type of information."

"I didn't pay you to think. So right this second you have nothing? And I've spent three grand for you to so thoroughly follow a woman to her car? Wow, I hope you weren't seriously injured." With blunt sarcasm Mrs. Hamilton tore Shawnn a new one. As if he was so full of shit, he needed two assholes to expel excrement.

*Bitch,* thought Shawnn before replying, "Actually, I do have something. This woman will be at your husband's job tomorrow. He'll be meeting with the CEO Cedric Montgomery at 2:30."

"Finally something I can use," Mrs. Hamilton stated before she hung up in Shawnn's face.

*Double bitch,* Shawnn thought replacing the phone in its cradle. He didn't understand her motives behind this. Shawnn had told her that her husband was not cheating, but she still insisted on finding the woman. Maybe it wasn't meant for him to understand. It didn't matter. He would have an address to the woman's home soon and be done with the red-haired ice bitch.

A little while later Jasmine knocked on the door. It was 5:11. She was seeing if he needed anything before she left. He told Jasmine no. He still had not received the call he'd expected. Turning to leave, she reminded Shawnn, "Don't forget to take the Taurus home tonight. It's going to rain tomorrow." Jasmine always told him when the weather report called for rain so he wouldn't be walking to work when it did. But he had known just as he always knew. Shawnn could feel it in his bones like old people felt it in their joints.

"Alright. See you," he told her, then she left. Shawnn checked his email again before shutting down the computer. He still had no reply. Brewer still hadn't called either.

Shawnn lowered the blinds before locking and leaving the office. On his way to the Taurus he wondered if his night would be as crazy as his day. They usually were. Starting the vehicle he sighed; he was already tired.

# VIII
# FOLLOW THE MONEY

"So, do you believe that lying old biddy?" Thomas asked Wright on their way back to the police department.

"Not really. There's no evidence to support her claim. Plus I don't feel like doing the paperwork." Wright answered.

"It's not like you file any reports Danny," she reminded him using his first name. He liked the way it sounded rolling off her exotic tongue.

"Well, it could be true."

"Why? Have you been talking to her cat, her husband's ghost or the plant," Thomas said with a smile.

Wright smiled too before answering. "Actually, I found this." He pulled a small piece of white fabric from his inside jacket pocket and handed it to her.

"What's this, the contents of your wallet?" she asked twirling the thread.

"Why aren't we the comedian today? But no, it's what I found stuck in the splinters of wood in the frame of the window when I rechecked it. I figured if a man jumped, the window was too small not to have caught him or scratch him in some way," Wright declared.

Thomas was quiet a moment before admitting, "I believe her too." Wright didn't say anything so she continued. "You didn't notice anything strange when you looked out the window?"

Wright considered this, thinking of the air conditioners and a few satellite dishes. "No," he answered.

"Did you see the cable dishes?" she asked.

"Yea, so?" he answered.

"The one two floors under his window was falling. I know the owner didn't put it in that way because it would have been impossible to get any reception," Thomas said.

Wright thought about this a minute trying to visualize the scene and realized that she was right. "So what does that mean?" he asked.

"Could mean nothing. Or it could mean everything," she responded.

"Then where was the body?" They both grew quiet in deep contemplation. No human alive could have walked away from that fall.

When they got to the station Lieutenant Crump chewed them out about the precious man-hours they had wasted on that bogus claim that could have been used on the Hijinks Heist. Apparently Officer Brewer had told the lieutenant about their useless investigation.

Wright said that they were making progress—which was a lie. He also said that they had been interviewing the hostages again for leads— which was another lie. The truth was that they didn't have any leads to get or to go on. So what more could they do? But Wright had a plan, though he was reluctant to tell the lieutenant or captain. He told Thomas because he felt like a little pillow talk after the way he had dry-humped her all day. Thomas didn't think it would work. She said the criminals had been too smart so far to go for his half-brained ploy.

Wright figured that he would find out soon enough as he sat at his desk and dialed *The Atlanta Journal*. When all else failed, follow the money. Or in this case, let the money come to you.

Wright placed classified ads in not just *The Atlanta Journal*, but *The Constitution, Atlanta Advertiser*, and *The Gazette*. This was phase two of his plan. He had completed phase one yesterday, now all he waited on was the phone call that could lead him to the Hijinks Heist perpetrators. The news and classified papers had thought his ad a weird request that no one would reply to, but Wright knew that it was the only way.

Wright and Thomas re-conducted phone interviews at their desks of the available hostages. Afterwards they compared notes and were still no closer to the Hijinks Heist robbers. They called it a day at around 5:30. It had been a little more than thirty-four hours since the Bank of America robbery; still no suspects.

When Wright parked the deteriorating Crown Victoria next to the Bentley, he had a pang of longing. He thought he had neglected the luxury car and that it needed attention. So Wright decided on a night out on the town. He hadn't had one since. . .since. . . he fell in love with Veronica Thomas.

Well, Thomas would be the last thing on his mind tonight. It would be him and his baby; him and his car.

Wright clearly forgot that he was renting it. A self-deception that would end in heartache.

# IX
# NO WORRIES

At Trinity Enterprises a woman sat in her chair, pushed back away from her desk with her skirt bunched-up around her tiny waist. Her panties were around her ankles, and a man was on the floor in front of her with his head buried in her lap.

She moaned in ecstasy as the man used his tongue to taste the jewels of her treasure trove. The man ate her hot twat with wanton vigor. His tongue teased and turned her knob of pleasure. She bit her lip almost hard enough to draw blood as the man exhibited fine-tuned oral techniques.

When the phone on the desk rang, Toccarra was angry at the interruption because she was on the brink of her second orgasm. She would have let it continue to ring but she was expecting an important call. Furthermore, the man had stopped pleasing her.

"Yes," was her near breathless but angry answer.

"I have good news," said the voice on the phone. "She will be there tomorrow to see Cedric at 2:30." This was not the call she expected, this was better.

"Are you sure?" Toccarra asked. That news was double ended; good because they would know where she was, bad because she would be seeing Cedric.

"Positive," Mrs. Hamilton replied into the phone.

"Good work," Toccarra responded to Mrs. Hamilton and to Patrick under the desk as he resumed gorging on her waiting hot-box.

Toccarra hung up. When she did, Patrick stopped again long enough to ask, "Was that him with the wiretap results?"

Toccarra pushed his face back into her vagina responding, "No, but it was my new friend with the news that the girl will be here to see Cedric tomorrow." Patrick stopped again. "No, she doesn't eat my pussy as good as you do. Close, but no cigar. Now focus."

Toccarra pressed his face back into her orgasm oozing womanhood again. Patrick hadn't stopped because the news of the wiretaps hadn't come back. Nor was it because of the news that Toccarra was screwing Mrs. Hamilton—hell he expected that. Patrick had stopped because of the fear of having the woman they were chasing talk to the CEO of their company; Cedric Montgomery. She was getting way too close to the truth. Patrick felt Toccarra's grip tighten on the back of his head as yet another orgasm plastered his face with love juice. Obviously she wasn't worried.

# X
# PARKING LOT PIMPING
# TUESDAY, MARCH 8TH 2011
# SUNSET: 6:54 P.M.

It was late as KB exited Atl's famous Club 112. He had bought out the bar splurging and stunting hard, but now he was pissy drunk. He had even made it rain with large quantities of cash, throwing it up into the crowd as if he was in his own music video. Now he was ready to end the night with a thick snow bunny who had hopped his way. He walked with her as a crutch. They proceeded to his money-green 79' Impala on thirty-inch rims. Neither him, nor the female he was with noticed the man seated in the black car. But the man took note of them. One of them had the smell of death.

The parking lot was deserted because everyone was in the club partying. It was 1:32 A.M. Thirsty Tuesdays kept people with hangovers come Wednesday morning. The party was just beginning so the woman on KB's side knew they were alone.

Arriving to the driver's side of his car, the woman who had been helping him keep his balance kissed him hard on the lips in the quiet parking lot. "Slow down shawty," he said. The man in the black car watched with disgust.

"I'm taking you to the telly (hotel)," KB told the pale-skinned woman who was now kissing his neck. He tried to lean his right hand against the car for balance as he faced her. In the club it was dark, so she had easily hid her paleness. Now, in the light of the parking lot lamps and quarter-moon that was obscured by the gathering rain clouds, he could see her more clearly. She was kind of cute with long blond hair and a nice body. But she did need a tan.

*I hope she don't have that thang,* KB thought. *Fuck it, I'll just wrap it up.* He made his decision as he finally was able to find the keys to his car. They had been buried deep in his left pocket between stolen money.

The woman began to get excited as she kissed his neck. Her eyes went from light-blue to a solid black. Her fangs extended grotesquely. He didn't see this transformation but he felt the sharp pinch as she bit into the fleshy part of his neck. *Damn she's a freak,* he thought as he dropped the keys on the ground when he'd fumbled them from his pocket.

He bent to pick them up. When he did, the woman wasn't expecting the punch that connected square on her jaw. She stumbled back. Blood from KB's neck mingled with the blood that dribbled from her busted lip.

"Shadow-spawn," she hissed.

"Life-leech," the man in black snarled back before swinging another attack at her across the bent over KB. This time she was prepared. She weaved it and returned a staggering right to his chin. The man in black enjoyed the hand-to-hand combat occasionally, so he refrained from drawing the sword on his back.

With lightning quick speed the woman delivered a nice three-piece combination to the man in black's chest. She was ending it with a round-house kick just as KB was standing back up.

Apparently he stood too fast because he doubled back over and retched just in the nick of time to avoid being decapitated by the kick. The man in black wasn't so lucky.

The kick dazed him slightly. He returned a knee to her gut, then a jaw-rattling uppercut. He had no qualms about hitting women because he knew they would kill him with no hesitation if given the chance.

She stumbled from the uppercut that would have knocked-out a normal man. KB finished regurgitating a large part of the Incredible Hulk mixture of Hypnotic and Hennessey he had consumed in the club. He stood up straight into a left hook from the woman. The man in black wasn't prepared for the punch or him standing so abruptly, so he couldn't do anything to block the blow.

KB fell unconcious to the ground inches away from the pool of greenish-brown vomit. The man in black grew tired of playing games with the female vampire and said, "Say goodnight." Then his whole body burst into flames. As he did, so did she. But she smoldered before turning into a pile of gray-black ash.

The man went back to normal. None of his clothing was burned or even singed. He leaned over and checked KB's pulse. He was still alive. The man figured someone from the club would find him. He went back to his car to see if he could slay more creatures that go bump in the night.

# XI
# KNIGHT ON THE TOWN

THE BENTLEY UPLIFTED DETECTIVE WRIGHT'S SWAGGER. THOUGH HIS CLOTHES weren't up to par with how he felt, you couldn't tell him he didn't look like a million dollars—or at least a quarter of it.

He had gone to Magic City but refrained from drinking and tipping the strippers, so he was thrown out. That did nothing to dampen his mood. He was out to find a girl tonight and he wasn't going to pick up any prostitutes either. He wanted someone who was not just hip, but classy like Thomas, so he didn't visit any of the bars he usually frequented. For the first time in all of his years in Atlanta hearing about it but never going, he graced Club 112 with his presence.

He had been enjoying the purr of the Bentley's 622 horses, slowly cruising the city when he had made the decision. It was almost 2:00 by the time he pulled into the crowded parking lot. If it was like this on a weekday he couldn't imagine it on the weekends.

He cruised the parking lot attempting to show off his coupe but there was nobody out there to stunt for. Everyone was in the club. On his final stretch he saw a man lying face down next to a green car on big rims. He probably would not have noticed if the car wasn't sitting so high off the ground.

Wright pulled over to examine the man. He was out cold, but still breathing. *He must have had way too much to drink,* Wright thought smelling the stench of the puddle of throw-up. Wright saw the pile of dust on the ground; as if someone stood there smoking a hundred cigarettes.

Wright rummaged in the man's pockets. There was some money wrapped in rubber-bands, but he found no ID or wallet. He checked his back pocket and found a single prepaid visa card with a Georgia driver's license. The man's name was Kelby Blakely. Wright tried to wake the man but he was too far gone. Knowing he couldn't leave the man, Wright called an ambulance to the scene. His night on the town was officially over. Omen?

# DAY THREE

# I
## DRENCHED SPIRITS
## WEDNESDAY, MARCH 9<sup>TH</sup> 2011
## SUNRISE: 7:33 A.M.

Turning off the alarm, Shawnn proceeded with his usual morning routine. After completing his Tai Chi forms and taking a shower, he dressed in a stylish custom pinstriped suit. He took his clothing serious. He dressed immaculately knowing that it was going to be a light day filled with office work.

He looked out of his bedroom window at the light drizzle and wondered if the sun would come out from behind the rain clouds at any point during the day. The rain drenched his mood just as it drenched the streets.

While eating a strawberry toaster strudel, Shawnn sat at his kitchen table reading Sun Tzu's "The Art of War." Since not having to walk to work gave him some extra time this morning, he occupied it by catching up on his enlightened reading.

*Crush your enemies fully,* Shawnn thought. *That's exactly what I plan to do.*

# II
# HANGOVERS AND HARD-ONS

WHILE SWIMMING THROUGH THE MURKY WATERS OF UNCONSCIOUSNESS THE ALARM alerted Wright that he needed to come up for air. He'd had a late night but was thankful he didn't partake of the sinful drink; no headache. But he was not thankful he didn't partake of the sinful woman; he awoke with a hard-on.

He washed away the lingering effects of his lustful dreams and prepared for his day. Leaving, the Bentley once again looked at him as if betrayal. Driving the Ford he felt that last night he betrayed himself.

# III

# PATIENCE

Shawnn arrived at his office to find Jasmine at her normal post. He settled into his desk and checked his e-mail. Still no reply. He started on *The Atlanta Journal* while for waiting on Officer Brewer to call.

Shawnn prepared two files he had neglected due to the Hamilton case. Most of them just took a little internet research. Everything was easy. Tired of waiting, Shawnn made a call but got no answer. He normally could count on Brewer, he didn't understand what was going on. He was supposed to have given him the address to the tag yesterday. Puzzled about this, Shawnn returned to doing the research.

At 11:30 he went to Burger King on 4th Street for lunch. He ordered himself a Double Whopper with cheese value meal and two 5-piece chicken strips with a Hershey's pie for Jasmine.

When he returned with the food, Jasmine handed him a sticky note with a message from Officer Brewer on it.

*He would call as soon as I leave*, Shawnn thought reading the neatly scrawled note. It read: Kellie McCormick, 425 Howard Street Buck Head. Smiling, Shawnn grabbed his Cannon camera from his office before heading out the door.

# IV

# DONATIONS

THE SMELL OF ANTISEPTIC WAS STRONG AS THOMAS AND WRIGHT ENTERED THE
Red Cross blood bank in downtown Atlanta. They always donated blood
at least once a month. They felt it was their civic duty. Thomas' mother
died because the rare O-negative blood type wasn't in abundance at the
time she needed a transfusion.

Wright and Thomas sat in the lounge filling out the necessary paperwork. There was a movie on but neither of them paid it much attention. They were surrounded by a lot of different people but most of them
were bums or crackheads.

To promote donations the Red Cross gives anywhere from thirty to
fifty dollars per pint of blood donated. For some this was a means to a
hit for the day, for more it was a hot meal.

After turning in their papers and a brief physical with a nurse that
proclaimed him fit to give blood, Wright was escorted to the back of the
blood bank. Thomas was still waiting on her physical.

The rear of the blood bank had twenty seats; ten on each side of a
partition. Five on the walls to the left and right and five back to back
on the center partition. These seats resembled dentists' chairs. They re-
clined the donor back comfortably so they wouldn't pass out from the
rapid loss of blood. Sixteen of these chairs were filled. Between these
seats were large consoles that resembled ATM machines.

A technician in a white lab coat that had the Red Cross insignia on it escorted Wright to a seat near the rear. Her name was Amanda; Amanda Frasier. Wright would never forget that name as long as he lived.

Amanda was cute but somewhat chunky. She had long curly blond hair. Her eyes were a sparkling shade of turquois and her chubby cheeks fit her face nicely. She seemed to have a sunny disposition and outlook on life. As she escorted Wright to his seat they passed other technicians, but none seemed to enjoy their job like Amanda.

At his seat they chatted while Amanda prepared the necessary tubes, hoses and equipment to steadily withdraw blood. She hooked him up to the ATM-like machine with robotic thoroughness.

"How long have you been working here?" Wright wondered.

"Three years and I love it," Amanda replied.

"Why? You're around other people's blood all day." Wright pressed.

"It's not their blood it's the people. Most people are nervous, scared of needles or whatever. I get to comfort them and also meet lots of new people every day. I feel like we each have a special bond together because I draw their blood. It's what gives life." She tore open an alcohol pad and rolled up Wright's sleeve as she talked. "Oh, you have nice arms and smooth veins. You can tell a lot about a person from their veins. It looks like you're under a lot of stress."

Wright studied his arm wondering how she could see that. She tore off strips of tape that she was about to use and continued, "I can tell you are in public service. Probably a fireman or police officer."

Wright flinched at this assessment, giving her confirmation.

"Oh, so a police officer huh. Judging by your suit and I-don't-give-a-damn attitude I'd say you were a homicide detective."

Amanda took the needle and stuck it in his arm before he even realized what she was doing. She did it so swift he didn't even feel any pain.

"Yeah, I can see it in your eyes. Whoever you lost drove you to this job so that you could control the outcome of other cases. You want vengeance for your loss so you extract it by giving vengeance to others through finding their loved one's killers." She had an unnaturally calming quality in her voice. And until she had analyzed him he never realized why he was who he was. Amanda was right.

"All done," she replied after taping the needle in place on his arm. "I'll be back in around twenty minutes. Just holler if you need anything."

With that, she left him to enjoy the near silent hum of the machine as it drew his blood in slow intervals. Once again he sat facing a television, but his mind was too far removed to recognize or relate to the pictures on the screen. Wright was lost in the thoughts and memories of his mother and father—the reason he became a homicide detective. Wright planned on thanking the technician—Amanda Frasier—for her analysis and giving him a little understanding to his life. Wright would always be sorry that he never got the opportunity.

# V
# GOOGLE GUESSING

Shawnn approached the address located in the suburban area of Buckhead. The house was a two-story Victorian with a modern stone facade. Sure enough a navy-blue Impala was parked ostentatiously in the driveway. Shawnn crept by seeing what appeared to be the brunette—Kellie McCormick—in a red kimono in the living room. She seemed to be working out or doing some type of exercise. Shawnn couldn't make it out while simultaneously focusing on the road. He took three candid photos and then circled the block taking four more. He decided that was enough, so he proceeded to head back to SPI.

When he got back he went into his office and retrieved a small memory stick drive from his desk. Next he opened a compartment in the camera he had just used and removed a similar memory chip.

Shawnn gave both of them to Jasmine with instructions to have them developed asap. When he went back into his office he logged onto the internet and did a Google search on Kellie McCormick.

Shawnn was amused but not surprised to find out that she was twenty-eight and had two degrees; one from Princeton, one from Harvard. One degree in psychology, and one in modern history. What surprised him was that her life didn't seem to start on paper until she graduated from Colonial High School in Lexington, Kentucky. There was nothing on her before then. No birth place, no awards, no arrests, not even anything on her parents. It was as if she appeared the day she graduated.

Even more perplexing was the fact that upon further research, Shawnn found out that Colonial High School closed in 1913. He printed what information he thought useful and prepared a file for Mrs. Hamilton. He was glad to be finished with her and her deception, but even more curious about whom Kellie McCormick really was.

# VI
# RED CROSS UP

Wright was relaxing as he relived fond memories of his childhood with his loving parents when a loud commotion brought him back to the present, forcing him to close his mental photo album. He slowly opened his eyes taking in the scenery. He had almost forgotten he was in the blood bank.

Wright sat upright in his seat as the ruckus grew louder. It was coming from one of the storage areas so Wright couldn't see what was going on. From the distraught cries and noises of things being knocked around it didn't sound good. Wright knew he had to help. Whatever was going on wasn't in the normal operating limits of the Red Cross. No technicians were around to help. They must have all been aiding and assisting in the trouble that was afoot. Wright did not understand how to stop the machine or turn it off. He should have been paying more attention when he was being hooked up to it, but he was too entranced by Amanda Frasier's eyes and voice. The other donors looked nervous.

Wright pressed a series of buttons on the machine's numeric keypad but none of them stopped or even slowed the machine. It continued to draw blood in the same steady pace while the commotion of the storage area grew louder.

Wright decided to unplug the machine but the machine was positioned so that its heavy base prevented access to the socket. In a last ditch effort he pinched the hose off that was inserted into the needle in his arm then pulled it out quickly. Only a small amount of blood dripped from the needle as the tube that was filled with Wright's red blood was replaced with the air of the room. The machine screeched loudly at this violation just as Wright was unstrapping his arm.

At that moment a medium-sized, pale-skinned man burst from the storage area. He held a bag of red liquid up to his mouth, sucking from it in one hand. In the other, he wielded a switchblade. Wright was shocked when he realized what was in the bag.

The average seventy kilogram human body possesses five liters of blood. Of that forty-five percent is cells, the rest is plasma. Plasma is a chemical soup made up of ninety-five percent water, the rest is proteins, electrolytes and nutrients. The red blood cells are what carry oxygen. It is the protein hemoglobin packed within these disk-shaped cells that make our blood red. This same protein is what the man with the switch-blade was gorging vehemently on.

Wright couldn't believe his eyes. He stood, pulling his pistol from its holster and pointing it at the man. He yelled, "Freeze!" The other patrons of the blood bank watched this episode unfold as their lifeblood was sucked from them voluntarily; not by man, but by machine.

The man, psychotic as he appeared to be knew he couldn't win with a knife in a gun fight, so he randomly chose a hostage. Whether if by fate or bad luck, Amanda Frasier was rounding the partition where the man stood. To this day Wright wonders if she was coming to check on the commotion from the storage area or if she was checking on him because his machine was beeping. He wonders if he could have saved her had he not intervened. He wonders if instead of jumping the gun—no pun intended—as he always did, that if he let the events unfold would he have by inaction saved Amanda Frasier. Wright would never know. But what he knew at the time, and still does is; knowledge without action is impotent, just as action without knowledge is reck-less. So for him to have sat with the knowledge that he possessed would have been impotent. But without knowledge of the full situation his action was reckless!

The man grabbed the unprepared Amanda so quickly that she didn't even have time to scream before the knife was at her throat.

"Let her go," Wright yelled.

"Put down your gun muthafucka!" the man with the knife returned.

"We don't have to do this," Wright pleaded.

"Yes we do. They made me like this and expect me not to live. I have to do this. I don't want to take a life every day just so I can survive another one," the man explained. But Wright didn't understand or have any idea what he was talking about.

"Listen, whatever the problem is we can fix it. I'm sure it can be worked out," Wright said calmly, still trying to defuse the situation. Wright's pistol was still leveled at the man but he was holding Amanda in front of him as a shield. Her broad body covered his well. The only thing visible on him was his face. It was right next to Amanda's, resting on her shoulder with the knife pressed against her throat.

"Yeah, it can all be worked out can't it," Amanda echoed Wright's words with no fear whatsoever in her voice. Her lips slowly parted giving Wright a smile that suggested she knew everything was going to be alright with her life in his hands.

The maniac with the knife must have felt her smile form from her chubby cheeks pressed against his because when she did, he said prophetically, "Yea, everything can be worked out—with blood." Then he too smiled just before he slit Amanda Frasier's—the technician with the sunny disposition and life altering analysis—throat.

The blood gushed out of the gaping wound. Before her almost lifeless body hit the ground Wright put three slugs into the man's chest. He spun as the force of the bullets turned his body like a top. Facing the other direction now, the man ran to the front of the blood bank. The bullets didn't seem to faze him.

Wright yelled, "Somebody call an ambulance," as he kneeled next to Amanda. He gripped her hand. She squeezed back but only for a second. She was trying to say something but every time she opened her mouth, only blood came out. This only lasted a second. Wright rubbed her cheek attempting to comfort her with his words of endearment. Fourteen seconds later she gave up the ghost. Wright was looking her in the eyes as she did. She smiled, and that smile stayed on her face even in death. She bled out while surrounded by blood she had help harvest.

For the first time in all his years as a homicide detective Wright cried for a victim. He usually stayed detached from the cases not letting the pain of death and loss get to him. But Amanda Frasier, with her openness and love of life, got to him.

As she said, when you draw someone's blood you take and see what gives them life. You form a special bond with them. And within a span of fifteen minutes this bond had been formed and broken.

Wright gently laid her head down on the tile floor of the blood bank then he went to pursue her killer. His tears dried quickly from the heat of anger.

# VII
# A PAIR OF PRETTY EYES

"My successor will be named a week from Monday just as we unveil the N-1000 and rid ourselves of any unwanted resistance for good. It's been a long time coming, but I'm finally ready to enjoy the rewards of a lifelong crusade Patrick." Cedric Montgomery said this with a solemn look on his face. He and Patrick Brewer were in his office having this discussion.

"It's about time," returned Patrick. "I've let you reign long enough. Our families' sect is—"

Just then Montgomery's secretary Tennia buzzed-in with, "Your 2:30 is here Mr. Montgomery."

Montgomery glanced at his expensive gold Rolex. The time was 2:26. "Send her in," he replied.

After arriving at Trinity Enterprises and going through a search that did everything but ask for a urine sample, Kellie McCormick AKA Marlana McDonald was finally being led into the meeting. As the secretary escorted Ms. McDonald into the office a tall skinny man in a suit passed her on his way out.

The walls were carved with architectural paneling which was brightened by modern frontier art. The paintings all looked to be originals. The panel walls were topped with ornate white moorings and a white dome ceiling. The floor was bleached oak over which sat an ornate oriental rug which looked handmade and original. In a corner sat a Chippendale's table holding a China tea set. The rest was a standard high paid CEO's office: oversized desk and leather chairs. Diplomas, photos and plaques lined the wall in a tribute to the owner's success.

"Cedric Montgomery, Chief Executive Officer of Trinity Enterprises," the man introduced himself, drawing Ms. McDonald from her observations. He extended a hand.

"Marlana McDonald, freelance journalist," returned McDonald, accepting the offered hand. As Montgomery shook her hand he studied her with a gaze so intense she felt naked. His eyes pierced her, leaving her with a stabbing feeling that Mr. Montgomery was very dangerous.

He was dressed in a custom three-piece Armani suit with matching handmade Italian loafers. His chest seemed to bulge on either side of his Hermes tie.

"Have a seat," he motioned at the leather couch taking a seat next to her. "I hear you're seeking information on 'The Great One'," he said using air quotations for emphasis.

"You heard correctly Mr. Montgomery. What can you tell me?" she answered, glad to not be distracted with small talk.

"Well, what exactly do you know?" Mr. Montgomery asked.

"What you can tell me depends on what I know? Interesting. In that case I know enough to believe without a shadow of a doubt that he's in Atlanta as we speak." McDonald informed him.

"What draws you to that conclusion?" he mused.

"A number of irrefutable facts from reliable sources," was her vague response.

"So why do you need this 'information'?" was Montgomery again with the use of air quotes while raising a suspicious eyebrow. McDonald was now convinced that he knew some, if not all about what she needed to know. She too was very observant and skilled at the art of reading body language.

"I'm doing an article for *Time Magazine* on the five most known, but unknown richest men in America. Gregory Cosby AKA 'The Great One' is number two," she explained.

"Second to whom?" Montgomery was curious.

"Bill Gates of course." McDonald felt scrutinized as Montgomery studied her for a moment with those intense eyes. They were almost the same shade of green as her's.

He was saying, "Well Ms. McDonald, I can't—"

McDonald interrupted, "Call me Marlana."

"Fine, Marlana." He continued, "I would love to help you but there's nothing to tell. Gregory Cosby is a myth—a ghost. He's a figment of imagination for the people who believe in him."

She replied, "I believe in ghosts Mr. Montgo—"

"Cedric."

She smiled coyly. "Cedric, I have reason to believe that you know he exists and know him personally. So if you plan to sit here and play games with me I won't allow you to waste anymore of your time or mine." She said this as she stood up to leave.

*Well I tried,* Montgomery thought. Standing up he said, "Sorry. I should have known better then to have insulted your intelligence by using that ruse. Not every day do I deal with someone as well put together as you. Allow me to apologize over dinner. We will be able to trade notes and discuss 'The Great One'."

*Men,* she thought. *So pliant and predictable over a pair of pretty eyes!* "Okay," she accepted reluctantly. "When and where?"

"The downtown Benihana on Friday. Leave me your address and I'll have my driver pick you up in the company's limo around 9:00," he offered brandishing wealth.

"I believe I can manage my own transportation. I'll be there by 9:30," she responded offering her hand for a deal sealing shake. He took it. As she went on the upward motion he slowly drew it up to his cool lips, giving her hand a firm yet soft kiss.

Unprepared but not surprised by this act she retrieved her hand and turned to see herself out of his office.

Harold Hamilton had called and tried to warn her off of the meeting the night before but she was now glad that she hadn't taken any heed to his assessment of danger. Mr. Montgomery was in wonder of where he had seen her eyes.

Watching her hips sway and that nice plump ass as she departed, he replayed the brief meeting he'd just had. He had been fully prepared to deny any and all rumors of 'The Great One' and dismiss her just as quickly. But that was before she sauntered into his office with that tiny skirt and big. . .brain. He could ignore a physical attraction but he just couldn't resist the air of unlimited intelligence she radiated. Plus her eyes were so familiar, he just couldn't place them at the moment.

In setting up a dinner date he wanted to assess the information she had before deciding on a definite course of action. He needed time to recall where he had seen those eyes. But he knew people who asked about 'The Great One' didn't ask for long.

Pressing a button he spoke into the receiver on his desk, "Tennia, call *Time Magazine* and get me any information you can on one of their journalist—Marlana McDonald."

⌒⁊⥎⌒

"She's leaving the building as we speak," Patrick said into the phone.

"Is there a tail in place?" the woman asked.

"Yes, Anthony's on it," Patrick replied.

"Excellent," Toccarra exclaimed hanging up the phone.

# VIII
# NO NEXT TIME

WRIGHT WAS HOT. HE WAS GOING TO CATCH THE CRIMINAL WHO HAD KILLED Amanda Frasier and have him brought to justice by the courts—that was if he didn't deliver the justice himself. Wright was more disappointed than shocked when he entered the lobby from the back of the blood bank to find Thomas with her knee in the man's back. He was on the floor face down. She had apprehended the killer and put the handcuffs on his wrists.

Apparently Thomas had heard the commotion but she was waiting to help Wright if need be. That was until she heard the gunshots. When the man fled she was waiting on him with a chop to the throat, then a knee to the solar plexus once he doubled over. Next she grabbed the hand that wielded the knife and flipped him over her shoulder onto his back proclaiming, "Gotcha." It happened too fast for the killer to put up much fight.

Wright entered the scene just as she was rolling him over onto his chest and cuffing him. It took sheer willpower to resist the urge to beat the man up while he laid there cuffed and subdued. When they picked the dazed man up from the ground to escort him to Wright's car for holding until a squad-car came, Wright noticed that the man had stopped bleeding. His shirt had the blood and holes from his gunshots but the flesh was intact. Wright pointed this out to Thomas who was unaware. She dismissed it as being blood from Amanda and holes that were already in the man's shirt. Wright knew better. He knew he had connected with all three of his well-placed shots.

Wright and Thomas now sat telling the black-and-whites what happened so that they could fill out a police report. There was two of them, Thomas and Wright knew neither.

They were standing next to the ambulance as they gave their statements. One made a joke about two 'bank' robberies in a week. Wright's glare stopped his laughter. Meanwhile, the man in Wright's back seat raised all kinds of hell. No longer dazed from Thomas' attack and obviously not feeling any effects from the three bullets Wright had put in him, he had all kinds of latent energy. He rocked Wright's Ford from side to side as he kicked and head-butted a door.

The ruckus he made didn't faze the officers or detectives because they were used to suspects and criminals alike taking their anger and frustration at being captured out on their vehicles. The ambulance personnel who had been wheeling the deceased body of Amanda Frasier away were not.

One of them said to Wright, "Man that guy's about to bust out of your car and escape."

Wright, used to this calmly began explaining to the EMT that, "Our doors are reinforced for scum like him. That was a former police vehicle, so it has the same steel as a squad-car. That makes it impossible for any suspect to e—"

He was cut off as the rear driver's side door flew away from the car like it was jet-propelled. Everyone was confused until Amanda Frasier's killer exited the vehicle and ran full speed up the street.

Wright snapped out of his discombobulated state and began pursuit. Thomas was right behind him along with the two cops. The killer was quick and ran with fluid grace. Wright noticed that though the handcuffs were still around his wrists, they were no longer connected to each other by the multiple links.

The man had a five second head-start that was slowly growing as he sprinted down the sidewalk. The few pedestrians in the area got out of his way, scrambling and knocking each other down as if the man was a rampaging bull. Wright and Thomas were in his wake jumping fallen bodies, trash cans and other objects that the killer had managed to add into the foray of obstacles.

Thomas lost a few seconds when she stopped to help a woman with a baby that had been knocked down. Wright's gap closed to five seconds and Thomas was just a few more behind him. The police officers realizing the chase was frivolous had long since given up the foot pursuit and called breathlessly for backup.

The detectives grew tired as the chase wore on. Though they were in excellent physical condition fatigue was setting in. They were about to abandon the chase when they caught a break. At the next intersection the man blindly ran out into the busy street and was hit head-on by a Toyota pickup. The truck skidded to a screeching halt. The man, no more fazed than by the bullets from Wright, got right back up and continued running. His gap closed to three seconds.

When Wright reached the truck, the owner looked confused as Wright jumped on the hood of his vehicle to avoid the building traffic and continued pursuit. At the next block the traffic was moving east to west too fast for the man to run out into it again. So he turned left around the building against the flow of traffic. Wright was ten feet behind him on his heels. Thomas was six feet behind Wright.

The surprise came when Wright turned the block but didn't see the man anywhere. He was confused until he felt the wind of the large semi-truck fly by in the opposite direction. Wright turned from the breeze and saw Amanda's killer holding tightly onto the cargo gates of the passing big rig.

The truck was going well over forty-five miles per hour; so how could he have had time to latch on? Easy, the same way he didn't have any bullet wounds. Or the same way he completely kicked a reinforced door off of its hinges. Like how he had broken corrugated steel handcuffs. How he had gotten hit by a. . .

Wright came to a decision. He was not willing to let happy-go-lucky-Amanda's killer get away. He knew backup wouldn't be there in time. Wright wasn't going to let him get away.

Under State Statute 17_54_1§ v (a), an officer of the law can commandeer a civilian's vehicle during an investigation. Though Hollywood portrays this as an everyday occurrence it rarely happens in real life. For the first time Wright pulled his badge out and held it forward yelling, "Freeze" as a car flew by paying him no mind. The next car repeated this a second later not even slowing to ogle him in passing.

Fed-up and knowing that the killer—Wright had never considered him a suspect because he had witnessed the killing with his own eyes—was getting away, when the next gap in the busy road opened Wright stepped out into the street to force the next car to stop. Either the driver wasn't paying attention or he was too busy to stop for an officer waving his badge, because he didn't slow one bit. Seemingly, the driver of the old school Impala sped-up.

Wright held his ground sure that the driver would recognize reason. He stood there defiantly with his detective's shield raised as if it would protect him from the impending danger. The donk on thirty-inch rims was only a few feet from Wright now, moving at almost fifty miles per hour. It was too late to move by the time he realized that the car wasn't going to stop.

Wright was going to die. And Amanda Frasier's killer was going to get away. Maybe he would meet her in heaven; if heaven existed.

Just as the car would have came into contact with his body, crushing him in the process, Thomas pulled him back.

"Gotcha," could barely be heard over the passing car's horn. They fell into a heap on the sidewalk. Wright landed on top.

"What were you trying to do, kill yourself?" she asked pushing him off of her. "You knew I would save you. So you waited just so you could be on top of me." She was dusting herself off once she stood up.

The adrenaline from almost being killed flowed through Wright's veins as he panted, still trying to catch his breath from the pursuit. He stood now staring at the wake of where the truck with the killer in tow went. He still hadn't acknowledged Thomas or her lifesaving intervention. She stood next to him still catching her breath.

"We'll get him next time," she said. But Wright knew that there wouldn't be a next time. Not for him. Not for Thomas. And definitely not for Amanda Frasier.

# IX
# SEE YOU TOMORROW

SHAWNN WAS FINISHING UP THE HAMILTON FILE WHEN JASMINE KNOCKED THEN entered his office. The portfolio contained everything it needed except for the pictures Jasmine had developed.

"See you tomorrow Mr. Starr."

"Alright Jazz, bye," Shawnn replied, then she left. It was around ten after five. Shawnn gathered his things to leave, checking his email before he did. Low and behold he had a new message in his inbox. It read: 'Thursday, the tenth day of March. The eighth hour of the clock, prime meridian. 4357 Montveiw Drive, Marietta, G.A. —Antione'. Shawnn knew the area and figured Antione must be doing well for himself to live in that neighborhood.

Shutting down his computer, Shawnn couldn't wait for tomorrow. Lowering the blinds he caught a slight glimpse of the sun peeking from behind the dissipating rain clouds. Shawnn figured that if it did drizzle a little more it was well worth the small amount of the sun's radiance he would absorb on the stroll home. He left the office tired but uplifted none-the-less. He would need high spirits for the night to come.

# X
# WHAT DO I PAY YOU FOR?

"WHAT DO YOU MEAN IT WAS AN UNREGISTERED PREPAID CELL PHONE?" TOCCARRA asked into the receiver. "Those are the easiest things to listen in on!" She explained to someone who already knew. "Scrambled? Encrypted? What do I pay you for?" She finally hung up in Officer Brewer's face, tired of his excuses.

The phone hadn't even had time to cool off from the anger radiating from her grip before it rang again. "What?" She snarled into the phone.

"Boss, we lost her," confessed the man on the other end.

"How!" Toccarra demanded.

"She was more. . . stealthy than we expected," the man explained.

"More stealthy?" Toccarra echoed angrily. "How many of you were there?"

"Five," was his shaky response.

"So you're telling me that five specially trained Lunari Assassins couldn't tail a single white female," Toccarra asked rhetorically, astounded at the implications. She was almost yelling now. "What the fuck do I pay you for? There will be more than hell to pay. And that debt rests on your shoulders Anthony!"

She slammed the phone back into its cradle. Her white-knuckled grip relaxed. She took a few deep breaths before speaking into her intercom, "I need to speak with Heather Hamilton ASAP!"

# XI

# DELUSIONAL

AFTER HAVING HIS CAR TOWED TO THE DEALERSHIP AND BEING QUOTED A PRICE TO have it fixed, Thomas and Wright grudgingly accepted a ride from the officers back to the station. . . in the back of their squad-car. It was humiliating. Wright couldn't understand how criminals could take it; the claustrophobia, the smell of stale vomit, the stains of other peoples' last ride in the back.

When they arrived at the station the lieutenant tore off into them. First it was about being no closer to the Highjinks Heist perps. Secondly, Wright discharging his pistol in an enclosed civilian-filled business. Thirdly, letting the suspect get away. Lastly but not least, the lieutenant was fuming about Faqui Muhammad's release over a technicality. But that wasn't what popped Crump's top.

What had him on the brink of cardiac arrest was the nine thousand dollar rental fee of a Bentley Continental luxury coupe. The bill was sent to the DeKalb County Police Department in care of Faqui's high priced lawyer soon after his release. Wright and Thomas stoically took the verbal abuse. It included things like: 'reckless disregard for public safety' and 'unauthorized spending of public funds.' Also, 'renegade detectives on a binge.' He finished with threats to their jobs if they didn't get in line.

Wright didn't care much. At the moment seeing the blood skeet from Amanda's throat was still fresh in his memory.

Wright contacted Amanda's next of kin—her mother—and told her to come to the coroner's tomorrow at 2:00 to ID her body.

After Thomas filled out the necessary police reports, they both—for the second time that week—piled into her Cadillac and she drove him home. The stress of their day was clear as they rode in silence, both lost in their own thoughts.

When Wright finally pushed the smile of Amanda's face as her throat was slit out of his mind he wondered about the events of the day—the killer in particular. He had been shot, slammed, broke a door off its hinges, ran over by a truck and ran half a mile before jumping onto the bumper of a moving vehicle. Who, or more importantly, what was he?

"Who do you think that guy will be?" Thomas asked with her eyes still on the road. She must have been thinking the same things as Wright.

"I don't know. And I don't know if I want to know," Wright answered.

"Well the CSI guys will have a match on his prints sometime tomorrow so we'll know soon enough," Thomas informed him.

"So did they find the slugs to the rounds I fired?" Wright asked. Thomas didn't respond opting to focus on the road. "I take that as a no. So do you believe me now that I shot him?" Wright pressed. She still didn't acknowledge him. "I mean, you saw him kick off that door. You saw him get hit by that car and hop up like it was nothing. Why do you want to know who I think he is? What do you think? Hell, you even seen him—"

Wright was cut off by Thomas, "Do you really want to know what I think?"

Wright said, "I wouldn't be asking if I didn't."

"You will think I'm crazy."

"And that wouldn't be different from how I think of you now," he replied.

"I'm serious."

"Me too," he smiled. She didn't.

"Wright, I trust you and your judgment fully so—" she was interrupted by him.

"I can't tell. You—"

"Let me finish," she cut him off. "I believed you when you said you shot him. I just acted like I didn't because I wasn't prepared to share what I'm about to share." Her tone was solemn but spoken with a plea to understand. It seemed as if what she was about to say was hard for her so Wright didn't push her. He waited in silence until she spoke again.

"When my mother was dying she didn't accept the blood that would have saved her. She believed in voodoo and sprits and such, so when she told the doctors that she had been bitten by a vampire they didn't believe her. They said she was delusional."

Wright thought about this. He had minored in psychology in school so he knew a little about symptoms and psychosis. A delusion is a false belief that an individual holds despite evidence to the contrary. Paranoia for instance, is an unsubstantiated belief that others are trying to harm him or her. Any attempts to convince the person that these beliefs are false typically fail and may even result in further entrenchment of the beliefs.

Thomas continued, "I knew my mother. She was a little eccentric but she was far from delusional. So as she bled to death from uterine dystrophy while keeping the doctors from administering any lifesaving treatment, she told me of the vampire that bit her. And I believed her. I may have been young, but I was old enough to understand that she didn't want to live the life she thought was coming."

The car grew quiet. Wright didn't have a comment. He didn't want to make a joke or ridicule Thomas because she was serious.

"I told you that story—which nobody knows of but my father and I—to say this; before today I had believed vampires existed, but I had never seen one. Well that's changed now, because I think that man was a vampire," Thomas told him.

He finally got the nerve to ask, "Why?"

"First, you said he was drinking blood that he had stolen."

"Right," Wright agreed.

"Secondly, you shot him but he had no scars from it minutes later." Wright nodded. "During her short stay in the hospital my mother kept trying to tell the doctors that vampires had healing powers for themselves and humans. That's why the bite marks on her neck healed. Something about a healing property in their saliva that works even after the victim is dead to avoid detection."

"Ok," Wright replied skeptically.

"Lastly, how many humans do you know that could have done any of the things we witnessed? Kicking off that door, getting hit by that car? My mother told me of their inhuman strength and stamina. You've seen the movies. Just think about it. Think of the weird reports we've had here lately. Missing people disappearing without a trace. Officers emptying full clips into perpetrators only to have them laugh. People jumping from eighth floor windows and living."

That made Wright think of the old lady's claim yesterday. "Just think about it," she finished pulling into his driveway.

Glancing at the Bentley, Thomas said, "At least now you have a legitimate excuse to drive it to work. Ten thousand tax dollars put to good use."

"Twelve tomorrow," Wright said getting out of the car. He waved as she pulled away. He couldn't help it, but she seemed serious tonight. Wright just couldn't let himself imagine vampires roaming the streets.

# XII
# ASHES TO ASHES
# WEDNESDAY, MARCH 9TH 2011
# SUNSET: 6:55 P.M.

THE MAN IN BLACK PULLED HIS MATCHING VEHICLE OVER AS HE CAUGHT A WHIFF of the easily recognizable scent of his enemies in the area. It was 3:20 at night, and under the overpass of the freeway the man spotted four boys. They ranged in age from sixteen to twenty-four. They were spraying graffiti on the concrete structure that held up the overpass.

"Dude, so what happened next?" one of the boys asked.

"So they were on my ass now. I was still trying to heal internally from the gunshots. So when I came to the next block I turned. The pig was getting closer. But when I saw this big rig coming I knew I was saved. As it flew by I stuck my arm out and grabbed on. It was going about sixty so I dislocated my shoulder. But I was alright after I popped it back into place," the boy finished.

Another asked, "So why'd you do that hot shit in the first place?"

"Because I knew I could get away with it."

"Well, you will have to chill after your funeral," another warned.

"I know, but does it hurt?" Amanda's killer asked.

"Only the embalming part. It burns like hell. But the burial and stuff is easy. As long as you're not claustrophobic."

162

"Yeah, you'll rise from the grave in three days like Jesus." They laughed.

"So Matthew, you ready to get down?" They turned to the only member who wasn't officially a member of their gang.

"I'm kinda scared."

"Dude I'm telling you you'll love the power of being a—"

Just then one of the boys turned to face the approaching man in black.

"Hey look, it's Spawn." The other boys stopped tagging the concrete and talking amongst each other. Peeved that their defacement of property was interrupted, they turned and laughed at the first boy's wisecrack.

"What the fuck do you want," another of the boys asked.

"Revenge," snarled the man in black as he drew a long silver sword from behind his back. It would have been easier to kill them all by phasing but the man was low on energy; fatigued by the long rainy day. Also, using his sword would be a hell of a lot more fun.

His sword glistened in the half-moon light. Before either of the boys could speak another word or joke, he swung. In one fluid sweep, the silver sword entered the foul-mouthed boy right under his left arm, and exited above his right shoulder. Before either part of his limp torso hit the pavement, they had disintegrated into a thin ash.

Seeing this vicious attack, the boys scattered in every direction. They were fast, but not as fast as the man in black.

The man in black turned, and in one swift motion he severed the head of the boy who had made the Spawn comment. Before he returned to nothingness, the man had turned and impaled another one of the boys above his left pectoral muscle.

*Slightly high,* the man in black thought as the boy went down in a heap clutching his wound. As the last boy made his hasty retreat the man pursued him. The man in black knew nothing of Amanda's death, or that this was the man who had caused it. All he knew was that the boy was the vermin of the earth—and he was the exterminator.

Before Amanda's killer had taken four steps the man in black struck. He swung with the efficiency of someone who'd done just that for many years. Meticulously—with no wasted movements. The blade came into contact with the top of the boy's cranium and continued downward smoothly until it exited between his outstretched legs.

Still in the running motion, one half of the corpse continued forward while the other awkwardly leaned to the left. The first half hit the ground then bounced before turning into ash. The second half of the torso followed suit, though not as gracefully.

That ended Amanda Frasier's killer's life. No memorial service, no one to remember him. But he did return to the essence: Ashes to ashes, dust to dust.

The man in black heard heavy labored breathing. He turned to see the final boy still on the ground clutching his chest wound. As he approached the boy futilely attempted to escape. He crab-walked backwards on the pavement using his legs and free hand that wasn't clutching his chest.

*Stupid,* thought the man. *Why didn't he just get up and run?* Sniffing the air and only catching a lingering smell of silver, he realized why. *Damn, he's human.*

The man now loomed over him so he stopped his meager attempt at elusion. "Why were you hanging with them? Didn't you realize what they were?" the man asked heatedly. That's when he realized why the boy had stopped trying to get away. The boy had passed out from blood loss and was slowly bleeding out.

The man took his sword and slowly drew the tip of his left index finger along its precision sharpened edge. He did this until he saw the bright iridescent blood flowing. Next, he held the finger an inch from the boy's open wound on his chest.

He let his blood flow freely, dripping into the wound; saturating it. After a few gruesome seconds the cut on the man's finger stopped bleeding as it closed of its own accord.

The boy who had not been able to protest as the man did this now screamed at the top of his lungs. "It burns! It fuckin' burns! I'm on fire. . ." His hands came to his chest tearing at the ruined shirt he wore. When he could finally make a hole big enough to see the wound through the shirt he was astonished.

In the dim moonlight he witnessed a miracle. Not only could he see, but he could feel the wound in his chest slowly closing. It completely healed. The flesh looked as if it had never been penetrated. The boy gratefully looked up to thank the man, but he was gone. Ashes to ashes, dust to dust.

# XIII
# HALLUCINATIONS

WRIGHT SAT IN HIS TRUSTY RECLINER LETTING HIS TELEVISION WATCH HIM. HE WAS stuck on the events that had transpired that day. He wasn't sure what Thomas proclaimed was true, but he was sure something funny was amiss. Wright knew what he saw, and he knew that he was being rational. Disturbances of perception and thought process fall into a broad category of symptoms. They were referred to as psychosis. One of the most common groups of symptoms that result from disordered processing and interpretation of sensory info are hallucinations. Hallucinations are said to occur when an individual experiences a sensory impression that has no basis in reality.

Hallucinations may be auditory, olfactory, gustatory or visual. For example, a visual hallucination can be seeing a man shot in his chest when he really wasn't. In each case, the sensory impression is falsely experienced as real. But Wright knew it was real. He was far from hallucinating when he saw Amanda Frasier get her throat slit. Nor was he hallucinating when the door of his Crown Victoria was kicked off. He had the bill to prove it.

Was he suffering from a form of psychosis? No, but he was having a very hard time explaining what he had saw that today. He attempted to put everything about the day out of his head as he turned the television to TBS hoping for a good movie. He got one, but it was the last thing he needed to see at the moment.

A black man with a sword was slicing vampires, turning them to ash. The movie was *Blade. Yeah, that would happen in real life*, Wright thought. But the movie made him take heed to what Thomas had told him. It filled in the missing pieces to a puzzle of mystery.

When Wesley Snipes' character jumped from a high window after being shot and unharmed, Wright thought that there may be an infinitesimal chance that vampires existed.

*Well, at least they don't have a sword*, he thought.

Continue reading for an exclusive sneak peek at Deception: Noon Book I of The Solari Trilogy Volume II ....

# DECEPTION

## BOOK I OF THE SOLARI TRILOGY VOL. II

# NOON

# SINTARI SUMMERS

# DECEPTION

BOOK I OF THE SOLARI TRILOGY VOL. II

# NOON

SINTARI SUMMERS

# DECEPTION

## BOOK I OF THE SOLARI TRILOGY VOL II

### NOON

*For as long as space endures, and for as long as living beings remain, until then may I too abide to dispel the misery of the world*

-Shantideva

*When the sun is at the zenith of its power, I too am at the climax of mine.*

-Centauri

# DAY FOUR

# I
# DUST TO DUST
# THURSDAY, MARCH 10TH 2011
# SUNRISE: 5:34 A.M.

It was early. Way too early for Wright. Getting into the Bentley he was just realizing that the sun wasn't even up. He received a call to head to a crime scene under the Jodason overpass. There were three homicides or possible kidnappings to be investigated.

When Wright pulled up to the scene he was still shaking off the effects of the dreams he'd had; or nightmares. He attributed this to watching that damn vampire movie before going to sleep.

He parked his car, stepped out and ducked under the crime scene tape. He found the officer in charge, headed to him and asked, "What's the scoop?"

It was too early in the morning for pleasantries and he didn't give a damn what the man's name was. Wright to put it lightly, was not a morning person.

"The call came in that a kid was in the street yelling to the top of his lungs about being burnt. The kid's name is Carlos Hammonds," the heavyset officer explained. He seemed to have a disposition that suggested chronic constipation. But so did Wright this morning.

"Apparently the kid and few of his buddies were out here a few hours ago displaying their fine artwork. That's when they were attacked by a man dressed like batman. Get this, this man had a sword and sliced his buddies into invisible pieces."

"Sounds like a movie I watched last night. Any evidence?" Wright wanted to know.

"The CSI's are bagging up that gray powdery substance that the boy says are his pals' remains. And the spray cans should have the victims' prints. Whether they were kidnapped or murdered we don't know, but the boy's ramblings aren't helping us put it together at all," the large squat officer said.

"So how are you treating it?" Wright asked.

"We're not treating it at all. From the looks of your car you get paid enough to handle it yourself," the officer said heading to his squad car.

Another investigation for Wright's already piled plate.

Wright approached Carlos Hammonds; an ordinary looking teenager with black hair and a pointy nose. He was wrapped in a blanket from the ambulance, obviously still in shock. Wright immediately drew his pad and at once questioned the shaken-up boy.

"How old are you?"

"Eight—Eighteen," Hammonds stuttered.

"What happened?"

"I told the officers three fuckin times s—"

"Now tell me a fourth," Wright interjected.

"Me and my friends were tagging the bridge and—"

"No names?"

"I didn't know them that long."

"Go ahead."

"Jeremy told us the story of how this cop shot him three times and broke out of his car."

Wright had been half listening up until that point. Now Hammonds had his full attention as he asked, "Where was this?"

"Under the bridge," Hammonds said as if it should have been obvious.

"No, where was he shot at?"

"He said in his chest."

Wright was eager now, "No, where was the location?"

"A blood bank or something," the boy answered confused.

"What was his name?" Wright's interest was piqued.

"Jeremy."

Wright had heard this name but could not figure out where. "Continue your story. Where are your friends now?"

"That's what I'm telling you and those other dickhead officers. They're dead. You can sweep them up off the ground. See those piles of dirt, that's them! When the man with the sword came slashing everything moving they evaporated into dust." Hammonds was almost hysterical.

Wright was trying to figure out the boy's MO. Kidding aloud and thinking of the Blade movie, he said, "Yeah, like vampires."

The boy stopped shaking and looked up at Wright with an awed expression.

"So you know about them too?"

Wright, thinking Hammonds was referring to the movie said, "Yep, seen it last night."

The boy felt a burden lift. He now spoke in a hushed tone. "I didn't tell those pigs because I didn't want them to think I was crazy or just trying to beat a murder rap. But my friends were vampires. They wanted to turn me into one but I wasn't sure. Some of the things they said they did to survive, I wasn't down for."

This threw Wright for a loop. He decided to play devil's advocate as he conspiratorially asked, "So what was the guy that killed them?"

Hammonds considered this only a second then said, "I don't know. He killed them all in like ten seconds, but he knew they were vamps. When he realized what he did and seeing I was human, he seemed sorry."

"What'd he do to you?"

"I guess he stabbed me thinking I was one of them. I thought he would kill me but he didn't. He used his blood to heal me. I was almost dead but he brought me back. And it burned like hell."

"Where'd he stab you?"

The boy opened the blanket to show a shredded shirt. He pulled it to the side to expose smooth white flesh. "He put the sword all the way through, but now you can't tell it ever happened."

*Got that right.* Tired of fantasy land Wright inquired about Amanda Frasier's killer once more, "So where is this Jeremy?"

The boy pointed toward the ground where the CSI guys were working. "Right there. That pile of dust. He's gone."

"So where is the guy who did this?" Wright wanted to know.

"He was gone too. I don't think I'll ever see him again. And I don't want to."

Wright continued to question Carlos Hammonds well past sunrise. When he finally decided to quit, the crime scene technicians were packing.

He caught up to one, "So what do I write this as?"

"Well, there was blood in the street and a lot of dust or whatever it was. But with no bodies or full names for victims, we don't even have a crime. We can't even file a missing person report. We'll print the cans but even if we get a match, all that will mean is that those boys held the spray paint; unless you're charging them with vandalism. Otherwise, there are no grounds to prove a crime has been committed other than the boy's word," the CSI finished.

"So this has been three hours of good sleep wasted?" Wright asked.

"Four for us," the man said loading the last of his equipment. "We're not even going to waste our time doing a chemical analysis on this. And do all detectives make as much as you?" He handed him an evidence bag filled with a gray-black powdery substance before leaving. Wright didn't even acknowledge his question.

Wright dismissed Carlos Hammonds after getting his info because he had nothing to hold him on. Getting into the Bentley Wright wondered if the boy was as delusional as he was, or if there was any merit to his madness. The sun was now up and in full effect. It was 7:23 so he headed to the department; early for the first time. The bright side was that he may have a bag full of Amanda's killer.

# II
# FINALLY FINISHED

SHAWNN ARRIVED TO SPI AT THIRTEEN MINUTES BEFORE THE HOUR. JASMINE handed him a large manilla envelope along with her usual greeting and his newspapers. He then went into his office and reviewed his work.

The large 8x10 glossies of what he'd taken came out just fine. He lingered on the candid photographs of the brunette before placing the pictures in with the file he prepared the previous day. As if on cue as he placed the completed portfolio into his filing cabinet, Jasmine buzzed him to let him know that Mrs. Hamilton was there to see him unexpectedly.

"Let her in."

Heather Hamilton came into Shawnn's office looking much livelier than she did the first time; if not more pale. Shawnn hadn't raised his blinds.

"Have a seat," Shawnn told her as he seated himself.

She stopped him in motion to his chair with, "This won't take long," refusing his offer.

Shawnn could see his reflection in the mirror-tinted shades she wore. *Still a bitch I see*, Shawnn mused to himself.

"I just need to know how your investigation of that woman is coming along," she stated.

"I'm finished," Shawnn returned.

Hamilton looked peeved as she said, "I've paid you good money Mr. Starr to do a job. We had an agreement. And if you don't plan on upholding our bargain, I'm afraid I'll be forced to—"

Shawnn could have let her undue tirade continue but he wasn't sure if he was more annoyed or amused. He did not take too kindly to threats. So at that point he interrupted her with a raised hand. "Here is the file I've finished. It has the woman's bio in it. From High School to now. Her name is Kellie McCormick. She's a—"

"Do you have her address in it?" Hamilton interrupted him.

"I don't think it would be much of a personal bio if it didn't contain her address," Shawnn retorted, handing her the tan folder.

Suddenly ecstatic, she snatched the folder from Shawnn's hand then turned to leave. He kept his hand extended, willing her to shake on the completed deal. In the days of Yore, knights used to shake hands to make certain the haft of a dagger wasn't concealed in a closed fist with the blade hidden along the forearm. Hamilton must have had something even more deadly concealed because she ignored Shawnn's hand completely.

"If you wait a moment I'll have my secretary cut you a check for the remaining balance of your account."

"What?" Hamilton replied before realizing what he was referring to. "Yes, you may keep the remaining money. You have been efficient." She then left his building without a backwards glance.

*Rich bitch.*

Shawnn turned to raise the blinds just in time to see Mrs. Hamilton getting into a green Lincoln Towncar. As it sped away, Shawnn turned on his computer to catch up on the files he had neglected the last few days due to the Hamilton case. He was glad to be done with it. He prepared other portfolios for clients as he willed the day to be over. He was eager to attend the meeting he'd been waiting for in Atlanta for four years.

# III
# OOHS AND AHHS

WHEN WRIGHT FINALLY MADE IT TO THE STATION HE GREW TIRED OF RECEIVING the '*oohs*' and '*ahhs*' directed towards him and his rented Bentley. He eventually found Thomas at her desk poring over the files.

"You're early," was all she said, but with an extremely surprised tone. He told her what happened that morning. When he finished she simply said, "I told you."

Wright didn't know how to take this declaration. So he stood there peering over her shoulder. To make it simpler for him and to get him off of her back she explained what she'd been doing.

Apparently their talk last night drove her to do research. She pulled all the unsolved homicides and disappearances from the past six months. The unsteady stack of files sat on the corner of her desk. In hushed tones she explained to him the mysterious circumstances around most of the crimes. She was convinced that they were all vampire related; he wasn't.

Around midmorning, only a fourth of the way through the unsolved crimes, a CSI that they were familiar with—Bobby Ray—brought them the results of the AFIS (Automated Fingerprint Index System) search from the murder weapon the day before. The latent prints were lifted off of the switchblade handle that killed Amanda Frasier.

The person had a domestic assault arrest two years prior in Fulton County, but the charges were later dropped. This victim—as in most cases—chose not to testify. The culprit who the fingerprints belonged to was Jeremy Taylor; Amanda Frasier's killer.

They thanked Ray for the information, but before he left, Wright had another request. He produced the bag of dust from the earlier crime scene and asked that Ray personally analyze it in a hurry. He said he had a lot of work, but give him twenty -four hours and he'd see what he could do.

Wright was pondering where he had heard Jeremy Taylor before. He knew that the boy Hammonds had given him that name earlier, but he'd heard it somewhere before then. It hit him just as Thomas was pulling a thin file from the stack of unsolved crimes.

Jeremy Taylor had been reported missing just the day before. His landlord said the police told her to wait twenty-four hours before they could file the paperwork.

At 1:00 P.M. Wednesday, March 9th, he was officially a missing person. There was no mention of the eighth floor window he jumped out of. Wright now understood why. Not only did police turn a blind eye to the science fiction element of the district, they covered it up. In the file there was no mention let alone copy, of the neatly typed reports Thomas had done for their investigation of the old lady's complaint. This didn't surprise Wright, it gave him a different insight on the situation.

Wright could not believe that the same person that the landlady—Mrs. Spears—reported committed suicide, was the same man who he shot and chased halfway across town. He also did not want to believe what Carlos Hammonds told him about Jeremy Taylor. He didn't want to believe he was killed by an unknown, unidentified assailant in black.

Wright told Thomas to continue what she was doing. He took the thin missing persons file on Jeremy Taylor to his desk. It was fresh, so the contact information for friends, family and acquaintances were up to date. He would figure out if he was just missing or if Hammonds hadn't been hallucinating when he said he saw Jeremy turned to dust in front of his eyes.

He opened the file then picked up his phone. Some people hold fast to a false belief despite evidence to the contrary. They were delusional.

# IV
# TOO IMPORTANT

"Forty-three fifty-seven Montview Drive. And I don't want any fuck-ups tonight Anthony. This is too important," Toccarra instructed into the Nokia cell phone she held.

"Okay boss," Anthony said hanging up his phone. He began preparations to rid his boss of a troublesome nuisance. At least, that was the plan.

# V
# COLD JUSTICE

LIFE'S BIGGEST MYSTERY IS DEATH BECAUSE NO ONE ALIVE TRULY KNOWS WHERE WE go when we die. It could be to a better place. It could be to a place far worse than we in our limited imagination would ever dream of. Wherever that place may be, good or bad, Amanda Frasier was now there. All that was left of her was a shell of her former self.

Wright had been unsuccessful at finding Jeremy Taylor though the police more often than not turned and re-turned every stone hoping for a new lead. By the time he was abandoning his efforts it was almost 2:00. So he headed to the morgue for the most dreaded part of his job; body identification.

The day before, Mrs. Frasier had been completely distraught when she learned of the loss of her only child. She cried shamelessly, and Wright had done his best to comfort the middle-aged woman over the phone.

Today in person she seemed more in control. She shared her daughter's chunky disposition, but lacked the vigor for life that Amanda had expressed.

But it's hard to be all smiles when you're going to ID the cadaver of your only seed. She'd maintained her composure until the ME pulled the refrigerated shelf that contained Amanda Frasier's shell from the wall. Upon seeing the lifeless face she bawled.

In life Amanda had been so full of joy and sunshine. Now it seemed death not only took her essence, but also all the beauty the young woman possessed. With a nod Mrs. Frasier confirmed what Wright had known. It was protocol for the next of kin to ID the body but to Wright, technicality caused undue pain to the deceased's loved ones.

Wright didn't turn away when Mrs. Frasier openly cried on his shoulder. He comforted her, patting her on the back. He understood.

Wright was only thirteen when he came home to find his parents' bodies. Though their family was far from perfect he was still loved. It changed him when he found their mutilated corpses. His mother was a banker. His dad did not force her to work she chose to. She wanted two incomes just in case something happened to his dad. After all, he was a police officer.

His father had been a member of the NYPD; one of the toughest most respected police departments in America. And he was one of the best.

But with greatness comes jealousy. Though he had been a good cop, nothing he could ever do would shed the skin of hatred that his snakelike fellow officers wore. Rumors of bribes and excessive force had never been proven, but labeled him a criminal as if he'd been convicted. Still, Wright's father rose above it. He could have joined other police agencies but he loved what he did. This is what drove Wright to be who he is.

He modeled his career after his father's. The way he moved, thought, acted and talked. Though growing up he wanted to be like his dad, the true deciding factor was his parents' murders—Unsolved murder.

How could one of New York's finest be murdered in his home with his loving wife and the killer never be brought to justice? Everyday Wright and his aunt Helen—his mother's sister—whom took him in, went to the police station to see if there were any developments in the case. There never was. Just cops with their thumbs up their asses eating doughnuts.

Why weren't they looking for his father's killer? If they wouldn't, when he grew old enough he would. That became his sole purpose. It was why he became an officer of the law. To find his imperfect parents' killer. Not just to seek justice for himself, but anyone else who was being railroaded by the justice system. Though the move to Atlanta sidetracked him from his own plight, times like now kept it too fresh in his mind.

He still remembered the way his parents looked on the same type of steel bed in the same type of morgue. His vow to bring justice extended to every case he got.

Though it was hard to accept and even harder to believe, Wright admitted justice had been served.

When Amanda Frasier's mother asked if he'd find the killer, without a hint of irony Wright informed her that he'd been murdered earlier that morning by another killer who he was now looking for. It didn't taste like a lie rolling off his tongue, so when Mrs. Frasier accepted it to be true, so did Wright. He knew as everyone else did; justice was a dish best served cold.

# VI
# GLORIOUS DECEPTION

SHAWNN WAS PATIENT BUT IT SEEMED TO HIM LIKE TODAY WAS ONE OF THE LONGEST of his many years on the earth. He finally left his office at exactly 5:00 on the dot according to his watch. It was warm and sunny outside. No hint of the rain from the day before remained. He happily proceeded to walk home and prepare for his much anticipated meeting.

Just as the sun was setting Shawnn was getting into the shower. Emerging from the cleansing ritual, he headed to his walk-in closet. Parting the many cloths that hung there, Shawnn removed the faux-plywood panel he installed revealing a smaller cubby space. The space contained a few pairs of worn black jeans, a jacket and a long slender object. Shawnn learned a long time ago that even though he was extremely stealthy and quick, he was far from invincible. He'd had a few run-ins with the law so he knew firsthand how they operated.

That is why he kept these simple yet incriminating items hidden. It wasn't the best hiding place in the world, but it served its purpose and wouldn't be discovered in a routine search. If by chance someone discovered him or did catch on to his 'adventures', by then he would have had ample warning enough to get out of dodge.

Shawnn wore a black T-shirt so he donned a clean pair of black jeans—some were dirty with the grime and dust of the days past. Next he put on and strapped up a pair of black Nike Air Force One mids. Nothing fancy, just enough to give a little cover and still be comfortable enough to get physical in. Also a common enough shoe as to not be out of place anywhere. What was exotic though was the custom black leather jacket he put on next. It was long, sleek and formed to the contours of his body like a second skin.

What made the jacket unique was the custom area on the back especially designed to house the last item in the closet. His pride and joy, his heart of hearts; his sword.

Its name was Alpha. It was one of a kind, given to him by his mysterious martial arts master over seventy years ago. With that sword, Shawnn felt like he could do anything. He inserted the sword and scabbard into the customized place in his jacket and then he replaced the false panel concealing his devious items.

Now he was ready to face the night. By day he was cool, calm and collected. By night he was a vicious force to be reckoned with. What a glorious deception.

# VII
# CHALLENGER
# THURSDAY, MARCH 10<sup>TH</sup> 2011
# SUNSET: 6:55 P.M.

SHAWNN STEALTHILY EXITED HIS APARTMENT BUILDING AS HE ALWAYS DID. HE ENtered the parking area to find his second vehicle where he left it and had been leaving it every night/morning since upgrading to it. If his sword was his main lady, this car was his mistress.

It was a 2010 Dodge Challenger SRT 8. There were mild Challengers, the S.E. is standard with 3.5 liter V-6. The R/T packs the 5.7 Hemi, a V-8. But Shawnn being the car aficionado he is and never knowing when he may need to get light from a crime scene, chose the beefed-up 6.1 liter, 425 horse powered Hemi.

It hit him for forty grand but it was well worth it. It was triple black—black rims, paint and interior—with black five percent limo tint and a hide-away license plate.

Shawnn got in and started the massive Hemi. He didn't listen to the radio or police scanner tonight. He just let the rumble of the engine soothe him as he coasted through the calm Atlanta streets on his way to his destination.

Shawnn eventually pulled into the large driveway of one of the biggest houses on the block. Really, this house—more like mansion—had its own block. Shawnn had never been to a modern mansion, but he assumed if he had this is exactly what one would look like. Whoever lived here was not only doing well, but championship good.

Shawnn pulled up into the horseshoe driveway. There was a fountain in the middle shooting brightly colored water high into the sky. There was a five car garage to his right with one port open to reveal a Bugatti Veyron.

Shawnn got out of his Dodge and proceeded up the stairs to the large landing with the huge double doors. So anxious, Shawnn almost knocked before recognizing the doorbell. But before he did either, one of the doors swung inwardly revealing what on first appearance was a butler in a tuxedo.

"Mr. Sanders is expecting you," the butler said, but his mouth didn't move in tandem with the words he spoke. He directed Shawnn to come in.

The living-room and den were massive, centered by a Swarovski Crystal chandelier the size of a Volvo.

The floor was white marble speckled with gold flakes. The furniture seemed to be all antiques but Shawnn hadn't had the time to take it in. Nor did he care. In very jerky movements the butler led him down the corridor to the right. They passed four closed doors before the butler mechanically turned and opened the fifth one on the right side of the hallway.

The weird butler stood to the side after opening the door, motioning Shawnn to go in. He did so, and the butler closed the door behind him harshly.

Shawnn looked around to find himself in a large library. It had the most books he had ever seen in a personal collection, almost like a baby Books-A-Million. In the middle of the room sat a man behind a desk who upon seeing Shawnn stood to greet him. He too, was dressed in all black.

# VIII
## DIG YOUR OWN GRAVE

WHEN WRIGHT RETURNED FROM WORK HIS MIND WAS RACING. THE FACT THAT HE was driving the Bentley kept the reason he wasn't in the Ford fresh in his mind. He couldn't accept the fact that it was possibly a vampire that caused this havoc. It didn't add up. But in a sick twisted Bram Stoker type of way it did.

Thomas almost convinced him. But whenever you accept something as a possibility, that is the first step in believing that it could be true.

Wright called the witness to the killing of Jeremy Taylor to see what other information he could pluck from him. He was disturbed by their conversation. Carlos Hammonds told Wright that to fall off the radar and begin their covert eternal life, vampires faked their deaths. He said that—that was what Jeremy had been doing when he jumped from the window. He was supposed to stay on the ground and play dead all the way up to his funeral and burial. Then afterwards his three buddies were supposed to dig him up.

But Jeremy chickened out. He was claustrophobic and scared that his friends would leave him buried in the casket, doomed to an eternal life of darkness. Wright asked if he would suffocate, but Carlos said he didn't understand himself. How he took it blood sustained them, but as long as they were inactive they could live indefinitely.

Wright and Carlos Hammonds had a very colorful conversation that night. Wright wanted to file it away as science fiction but he had to admit some of it made sense; in an illogical, logical way. Kind of like being tickled makes you laugh but it has no effect when you do it to yourself. Wright found out that he wouldn't have to pursue the other boys' killer because technically, they were already dead.

Wright hung up the phone with more questions than he had received answers. But all of those new questions were abandoned when he received the phone call he'd been waiting for all week.

He smiled genuinely as he set up the meeting for tomorrow afternoon. He loved it when a plan came together. Especially one as deceptive as he had concocted.

# IX
# I AM OF THE LIGHT

"Do you understand why humans die?" the man seated behind the desk asked Shawnn.

Shawnn was caught off guard by this question. As a reflex he answered, "Because they age."

The man in black was in a lecturing mood. "But what is the reason they age?" he asked Shawnn who silently stood at the entrance of the library. The man not needing to be prompted continued, "Cells in humans get older and stop reproducing. Have you ever heard of telomeres?"

Shawnn watched as the man stood and came around his desk.

"I am Antoine, son of Jamell, son of Demetrious. I am of the light and the light is of me," the man introduced himself.

# X
# SURPRISE

THE FIVE HIGHLY SKILLED LUNARI LED BY ANTHONY APPROACHED THE WELL-LIT house under the cover of stealth and darkness. The moon was waxing as they crept up to the brownstone. They had done recognizance on the house earlier and with the information provided by Starr Private Investigators, they knew the woman living here was alone.

Three of them were scattered throughout the back lawn ready to strike the rear at any moment. Meanwhile, Anthony led the siege from the front.

When he gave the signal they all converged onto the house in unison, fully prepared to apprehend their target.

They were in for a surprise from the woman who awaited them in the house—but she wasn't...

THANKS FOR READING MY BOOK. AS A TOKEN OF MY APPRECIATION, HERE'S A FREE surprise from me to you.

Hope you enjoy!

# 90 DAYS TO LIVE

DO NOT CROSS THE LINE    DO NOT CROSS THE LINE    DO NOT CROS

## JASON NICHOLAS

# 90 DAYS TO LIVE

AFTER TWO YEARS OF BEING HELD AND THEN BEING CONVICTED OF A CRIME HE didn't commit, Jamal Gathers is released for a short period on a federal self-surrender. Upon his release he discovers a plot to turn his once beautiful and blissful hometown into a drug infested wasteland. As he delves deeper into this conspiracy, someone is also trying to bury him—permanently. The deeper he gets the more he realizes that his assailant may be one of the people he once knew and loved. Time is not on Jamal's side and the walls are closing in around him. His every breath is a blessing as he fights to survive his last 90 days to live.

THE *Beautiful* ONES

ANIKA
MALONE

# THE BEAUTIFUL ONES

No one ever said that growing up in Brooklyn was easy. Jackie, Renee, and Chan understand all too well what it means to be street smart. They have shared secrets and been there for each other even after experiencing things most girls their age should never have to deal with.

In a matter of seconds Jackie's world is turned upside down when her long-time boyfriend leaves to pursue his dreams and she's forced to face her demons.

Chan's slick mouth and quick temper isn't exactly the best trait to have as the girlfriend of one of the up-and-coming drug dealers in the projects.

Renee's reckless behavior pulls her into one dangerous situation after another.

Distrust and the allure of fast money will test them, forcing them to gather their resolve and forge on or risk losing more than just their friendship.

The emotional tailspin these young women find themselves in will challenge all they've known and will undoubtedly mold who they will become.

Three friends. Three struggles. And one summer that changes it all.

# VIOLENT VOW

As a child Eric witnessed the bloody execution of his father. With his father's last breath, he asked Eric to promise him that he wouldn't grow up to be like him. Eric was traumatized by this event and now has a reoccurring nightmare.

Eric grows up and pursues a career in law enforcement. He quickly excels and is promoted to detective. As a detective, Eric pushes the legal and moral limits in which he took an oath to protect. Along with his partner Jack, they are magnets to high speed car chases, police brutality and getting the job done by any means necessary in their pursuit of justice.

When new chemically enhanced drug called "Purple Passion" hits the streets, so does a mysterious crime wave. Eric and Jack turn up the heat on every snitch and informant to find out who's responsible for these illegal activities.

Soon the plot thickens and Eric's investigation reveals that some of the most influential and powerful people of his city are part of an underground secret society. Eric's relentless search for the truth takes him to places he never expected to go.

Before he knows it, Eric falls in love with a dangerously beautiful vixen. A twist of fate forces Eric to choose between his career in law enforcement and the love of his life. This split second decision will change his life forever.

# THE ABSOLUTELY TRUE ADVENTURES OF A TEMP GONE WILD

TAMARA WALKER IS TWENTY-THREE AND FRESH OUT OF COLLEGE WITH A MASTER'S degree in attitude, fashion and common sense. Thanks to her ability to excel in her modern academics, she is thrust into New York's corporate world as a temporary employee.

With as much control over her life as she has over her random job assignments, she has to protect herself in a world ruled by men. Armed with her exotic looks, charm and quick wit, she's destined to take over the Big Apple—but first she has to keep a roof over her head.

Tamara is notorious for having an uncanny knack of being in the wrong place at the wrong time. She quickly faces a world ruled by sex, drugs and corruption. This street-smart spitfire must learn how to calculate her movements in an equation of uncompromising positions and remain unscathed.

Tamara's adventures will either be her ultimate undoing or it will balance her out and be the greatest learning experience of her life. Only time will tell.

This deliciously wicked story of exploitation and sexual awakening will have you rooting for the underdog and laughing at her trials and tribulations along the way.

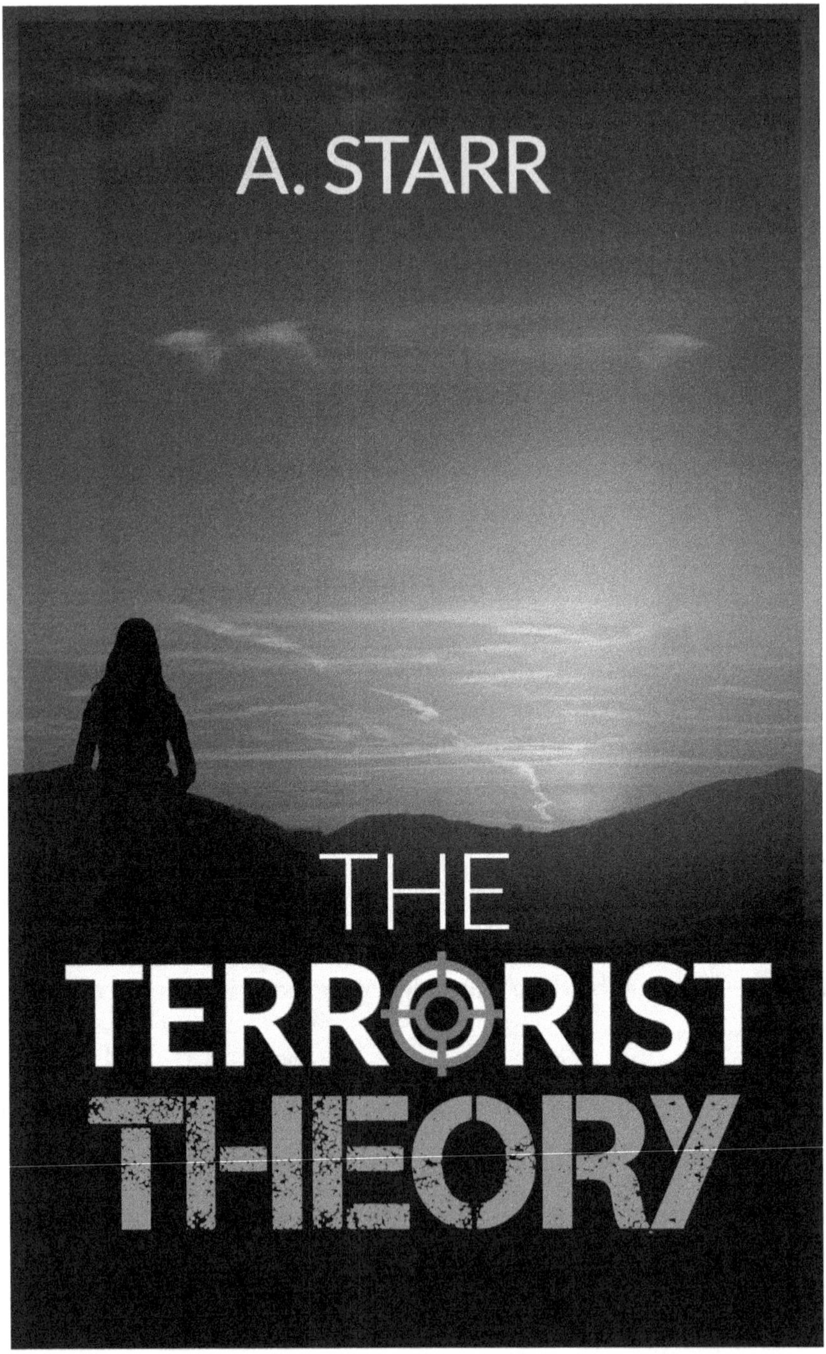
A. STARR
THE
TERRORIST
THEORY

# THE TERRORIST THEORY

Can you remember when the government was for the people, by the people? What would you do if the CIA kidnapped you and threatened the lives of your family with a strong hint at indefinite imprisonment if you didn't become a spy for them?

Charged with crimes of terrorism she didn't commit, 33 year old real estate agent Linda Terry was more than just a loving mother, loyal wife and caring sister—but she was far from a spy or terrorist.

While on a much needed vacation in Dubai, her entire world is turned upside down when she meets a mysterious man in a market. Soon after she gets abducted by the CIA who says she's now their primary suspect in hundreds of murders and killings due to her ties to the stranger.

Chained and tortured by the government that vowed to protect her, she is faced with two options; either she is condemned as a terrorist and doomed to never see her family again. Or Linda could cooperate and become the spy they want her to be with no training or background in clandestine operations. Then she would have to hunt the same man that had been eluding them for years.

With her family's lives at stake she becomes the unsuspecting spy, but what she uncovers changes her life and all the people she loves—forever.

Death, betrayal and action lace this non-stop thrill ride as a woman fights for her innocence, the fate of her family and the freedom of every US citizen.

# 10 Minutes Past Too Late

## Anika Malone

# 10 MINUTES PAST TOO LATE

"BAD GIRL," WAS THE NICKNAME THAT LISA MUNROE WAS BRANDED WITH AT AN early age. Although a successful attorney, this young black professional does everything she can to embrace her title.

On the surface Lisa would appear to have it all; a promising career, a committed relationship with her man Darnel Harvin and the prospect of more to come. But underneath the surface, Lisa's cynicism has caused her to believe that there is no such thing as a "long-term" relationship.

At the height of her indecision enters brazenly handsome New York lawyer Mike Wilson, whose forceful nature could destroy everything she has.

When her life becomes a tornado filled with love, lust and confusion, she spins out of control crashing into everyone around her. With the passion of one man and the pleasure of another, she finds herself backed into a corner and forced to reveal everything.

So what does a bad girl do? Does she rely on the old antics and tricks that have saved her in the past? Does the prospect of shattering the lives of the ones she loves force her to look within herself and confront some truths that could forever change her? With the support of her sister and her loyal overstepping assistant André, will they bring her back from the brink of self-destruction? Or for Lisa, is it ten minutes past too late?

Visit www.Starr-Publishing.com to sign up for our newsletter and receive a special gift from us.